S0-DQV-824

WITHDRAWN

Advance comments on
THE DANCE OF THE WILD MOUSE:

"*The Dance of the Wild Mouse* is a powerful statement of the
senseless separation from all things human and natural that
we often suffer in connection with terminal illness. It
portrays unusually well the dehumanizing process of the
modern acute-care system and brings the reader into the pain
experienced not only by the terminally ill patient and his
family but by doctors and nurses who are caught in it.
The young couple are seen isolated and suffering, almost as in
a myth or a dream-landscape. . . . The book is very touching,
very haunting, and sufficiently provocative that I believe it
represents a valuable contribution to the literature. I myself
am very glad to have read it."
    — *Sandol Stoddard, author of* The Hospice Movement

"An incredibly poignant novel."
    — *Paul Brenner, M.D.*

"Could be a valuable tool for those who work with the
dying . . . and a sharp prod in the skins of all of us who are
too busy ignoring the everpresent reality of our own dying."
    — *Harry B. Scholefield, D.D.*

WITHDRAWN

Daniel Panger

# The Dance of the Wild Mouse

Entwhistle Books
Glen Ellen

F
Pan
c1

1. Death - fiction
2. Terminal care - fiction

Copyright © 1979 by Daniel Panger. All rights reserved.

Cover design & art by Ann Cherryman.

Library of Congress catalog card number 79-51409
ISBN 0-9601428-4-3  hc
ISBN 0-9601428-5-1  pb

file under:  1)  psychology/death & dying/terminal care
             2)  fiction


Available from:     Entwhistle Books
                    Box 611
                    Glen Ellen, CA 95442

to the Honorable Morris H. Panger,
distinguished jurist,
humanist,
and loving father,
1883–1961

DRIFTWOOD LIBRARY
OF LINCOLN CITY
4333 S.W. Coast
Lincoln City, OR. 97367
996-2277

# The Dance of the Wild Mouse

WITHDRAWN

# 1

The man groaned and opened his eyes to the darkness. His heart pounded harder than usual and his body felt prickly and hot. For a few moments he wasn't sure if he was still sleeping. He searched the room for a dab of light. It was entirely dark; not a trace filtered through the heavy drapes. Confused, he pulled his right arm free of the blankets and forced his eyes to focus on the luminous dial of his watch.

"Two fifty-three." It took him several seconds of concentration and a number of eye blinks to read the time. "There's more than four hours left to sleep." He smiled to himself and was settling back into his sleeping position when a peculiar sensation inside his abdomen brought him wide awake and left him with a feeling that something terrible was about to happen.

"It feels like a little mouse running up and down inside of me." His pounding heart increased its force until it felt as if it had become swollen, filling his chest and forcing its way up into his throat.

"What in the hell is the matter with me?" he whispered, seeking comfort from the sound of his voice. "I swear to God, I can feel the scratch of its toenails." Even before the words had been formed they sounded foolish, and the foolish feeling was reassuring.

"Two fifty-eight." His eyes wandered back to the watch. "Must be a cold or the flu; it's been going around. If I can get a good night's sleep, I'll probably be well by morning. Well by morning, well by morning," he formed the words with his mouth as the tune of "Frere Jacques" ran through his mind. "Everyone gets sick once in a while. I'm no exception. If I'm not well by morning," the tune kept going on, running along with the thoughts, "I'll be well by the weekend." The whole thing became a jumble and he was starting to slip down the funnel of darkness, when the mouse increased its frantic run and began to spin inside. "I'm going to vomit! I haven't puked in years. I'll wake my wife if I do. I don't want to wake her, she needs the sleep." The nausea receded. "Thank God. I couldn't have stood vomiting. Nothing I hate worse." The man's face cooled as a light perspiration that had formed during the nausea attack began to evaporate. "I just won't go to work tomorrow." He nodded his head to emphasize his resolve. "If you get sick, you might as well enjoy it. I'll lie in bed and read, catch up on my reading and sleep a lot. I must have the flu. I feel as if someone beat me with a rubber hose."

The man closed his eyes and shifted his position several inches, bringing his body closer to but not quite touching his wife's. Very slowly, trying not to disturb the sleeping woman, he moved his hand until it rested on the lower part of her abdomen. The warmth of her skin soothed his palm and the good feeling ran up his arm and spread out through his body, easing its ache and quieting for a time his pounding heart. He felt the flow of life from her abdomen where the baby lay curled in its warm, wet cradle and he allowed himself to sink for a few minutes into a soft, safe sleep.

The pressure of her husband's hand, light as it was, was sufficient to pull the woman into semi-wakefulness. An increasingly great portion of her attention had been directed toward her abdomen ever since the onset of pregnancy. After the swelling started and especially after the baby began moving and kicking inside her body, she would constantly run her hands over her belly, lightly poking and pinching the skin, testing for little movements. Even when her thoughts were focused away from herself, her hands continued to be aware of her abdomen and her abdomen aware of her hands.

Had her husband used the same degree of caution in placing his hand upon her arm or breast or thigh, it is likely that the touch would not have awakened the woman; but all of her being stayed so constantly alert to the presence of the child within that the softest touch in the area of her womb was sufficient to interrupt her sleep.

For several seconds she hovered in a state of semiwakefulness, then forced herself fully awake as a wave of resentment at the imagined intention of her husband's gesture ran through her body. "He wants to make love to me!" She held herself absolutely still, keeping her eyes closed, taking particular caution so that her breathing continued regular and deep. "He mopes around all week and makes believe he doesn't notice when I'm being friendly, then in the middle of the night when I'm sound asleep he gets the urge. The hell with him!"

A stab of anger caused her breathing momentarily to lose its even rhythm. She wanted to push his hand away, but judging the best tactic to be the continued feigning of sleep, exercised restraint. "I know why he wants me now. It's because it's dark and he can't see me. I've noticed how he has been turning his eyes away lately." Even as these thoughts were forming, the woman began to develop doubts about their veracity. Her husband had been acting strangely for the past week. He had neglected her sexually, but his actions had not been limited to her. He had picked at his food and seemed to be drained of energy.

Suddenly the woman's anger vanished. The image of her

husband's moping, coupled with the stillness of his hand—it had not moved in several minutes—turned her thinking away from herself toward the man lying next to her.

"His hand feels warm, warmer than usual." Still cautious, she gently touched the palm of her left hand with the finger tips of her right. "It feels warmer than mine; maybe he has a fever." She tested the thought, then with a tiny shake of her head, rejected it. "We just can't afford to lose any money. If he stays home from work, they'll dock him. He hasn't been with them long enough to get sick leave." She shook her head again, this time with less caution. "We simply cannot afford to have any sickness right now, not until after the baby is born. I'll feed him a lot of orange juice and have him wear his heavy sweater under his jacket. Probably some bug that's going around. He's got good resistance. He's not sick—just fighting off some bug. His hand feels warmer because it's on my belly." To test her new theory she cautiously moved her right hand until it was positioned over her husband's, then gently brought it to rest.

The touch of her hand caused the man to moan in his sleep; he moaned a second time and shifted his position, bringing his entire body into close contact with hers.

"He's soaked!" The man's wet skin made the woman shudder. "He must be fighting off the bug—you always sweat a lot when you are getting rid of a germ." The woman half remembered some similar statement made by her mother years earlier. "It's when you don't perspire you have to worry." Having concluded her advice to herself, she lifted a corner of the sheet and gently dabbed at her husband's wet body. "You've been working hard," she soothed in a tiny whisper. "Mother will give you lots of nice orange juice and other good things and make a big fuss over you till you feel better." As she dabbed away, her whisper changed into a soft croon. Her body gently rocked back and forth, a movement

4

picked up by the bed, turning it for the moment into a giant cradle.

"I'm sick. I'm sick as hell." The man's voice broke through his wife's reverie and brought an abrupt end to her rocking and singing. "You woke me up with your damn moving about—and couldn't you find another time to sing? For Christ's sake, it's the middle of the night and my guts are all twisted around inside me."

The shock of her husband's words left the woman furious and on the verge of tears. She was about to let go the flood and "give him some of his own medicine" when he groaned again. This time his face was turned in her direction and she could smell his breath. It wasn't his usual night breath, an odor that for some reason she didn't find unpleasant. "Strong mushroom soup" was her description of it. This new odor was almost metallic, rotting metal. It reminded her of a dead sparrow she had once buried in her back yard and exhumed several days later. The memory filled her mind for an instant: The neighbor's cat that had dragged the dying bird into her yard. The fluttering of the broken bird's wings as the cat teased it. Her rescue of the bird and its death and how terribly sad she had felt. The ceremony of its burial. Finally, her curiosity to take another look and see what had happened to the little creature during the several days it had lain in the earth. Her husband's breath was the smell of the decaying bird. The fifteen years that separated her darkened bedroom from the scene in her parents' back yard had not dulled the memory of that odor.

"He's sick." The sharp image evaporated as she sat up in bed and placed the backs of her fingers against the man's forehead. "You feel hot—what's the matter? Is your stomach upset?" As she spoke, the woman made a deliberate effort to sound matter-of-fact and unworried.

"I've got a mouse in my stomach," the man mumbled.

Then he shook his head several times and sucked in a great lungful of air. "I mean it feels like a mouse running around inside. Probably some gas, but I can almost feel its little claws digging into my guts—what a strange sensation. Jesus Christ."

"Do you want to throw up?"

"Don't even talk about it. I'm trying not to think about it. Please don't say another word about it or . . ."

"All right, honey, I'm sorry. There's a lot of flu going around. You'll be OK in a few days. Lots of liquids and stay in bed. I've had it and I know how lousy it feels." The woman hesitated. "I suppose you'll have to stay home from work. They'll probably dock you." She sighed. "Well, it can't be helped." Then almost to herself but just loud enough for her husband to hear, she muttered, "It couldn't have come at a worse time."

"I'm sick and she only thinks about my being docked. Jesus Christ!"

"I didn't mean it that way, honey. You're a hundred times more important than any money. It's only I can't help thinking about the baby and how much it costs these days."

"Screw the baby! That's all you ever think about—the baby, the baby. It's my baby too. And what good will the baby do you if you don't have its father?"

"My, aren't we getting dramatic. You have a touch of the flu and you start sounding like a dying man." The woman hesitated, then softened her tone. "I'm sorry. I have no right to complain. This is the first time you've been sick since we got married. I'm sorry. Maybe you'll be able to get some over-time. If not," she shrugged to herself, "if not, we'll manage. You're right." She forced a girlish giggle that didn't come out quite right. "You are important—important to me, to the baby, and I'm sorry I've been treating you so mean." As a confirmation of her statement, the woman picked up the

6

edge of the sheet again and started blotting her husband's perspiration. "You stay home just as long as you have to and moth—," she caught herself, "and I will take care of you. If you still don't feel better in the morning, I'll call the doctor."

His wife's words and the gentle touch of her hand soothed the man and he allowed himself to sink back into the darkness. The ache in his limbs and the gnawing in his abdomen lessened until finally they were completely numbed by sleep.

# 2

The man was awakened by his wife's movements as she eased out of bed. Despite the darkness of the room, he knew it was morning. Objects that had been invisible during the night were faintly visible now and a thin pencil line of light framed the curtained picture window that filled most of one wall.

He lay very still, concentrating his attention first on his limbs, then on his insides. The distress of the night had diminished, leaving a slight afterache, an ache little different from the feeling he had experienced a hundred times at the end of a vigorous game of tennis or handball. The familiar dull pain was somehow reassuring; he was exhausted, but felt so much better than during the night. "I'll just take it easy today." He made a slight adjustment in his position, spreading out into the warm area where his wife had recently lain. "By tomorrow, or at the worst the next day, I'll be back to work." He smiled as he watched the outline of his wife moving softly about the room. "I'll let her baby me for a day, do her good, take her mind off the baby; she hardly thinks of anything else lately."

The woman moved past the window and her protruding belly was outlined for a moment. The man smiled again, this time showing his teeth. The safety of the dark room allowed him to smile more openly than was his wont. "It's funny how a piece of me is inside her," he mused. "A speck of my own substance is growing in her body and soon it will be another human being, another person."

For the first time he thought of the unborn baby as a human being. Up to that moment it had been an unreal thing like the rubber doll his sister used to nurse when she was little. A rubber doll that felt like flesh, that drank from a bottle, that peed, that said "Ma-ma" when you pushed its stomach, but was not real. Pretend real, yes, but really real, no. Up until that moment the baby had been pretend real. Now, perhaps as a result of the distress during the night, perhaps that together with the safe exhausted feeling he was experiencing, the baby inside his swollen wife became a real person; one who would soon be really crying and eating and peeing, one who before long would be walking and talking and going to school. The tumble of thoughts was more exciting to the man than any he could remember . . . the idea that a piece of himself was getting ready to be a living human creature, one that someday would be fully grown, that someday would be the only thing left of him after that shadowy time he called death. The idea was intoxicating and it danced inside his chest up into his brain like crazy bits of electricity. The electricity crackled and flashed throughout his entire body, and the mouse started to run again.

"Call the doctor!"

The woman stopped her puttering movements, startled by her husband's voice. She had thought him sleeping and, reassured by his sleep, had put his illness out of her mind. In fact, for the moment she had forgotten about him entirely and was wondering whether "it" would be a boy or a girl.

"I'm sick, sick to my stomach. Call the doctor. Call the doctor, please, honey. Maybe he can give me something to stop this damn feeling."

Almost as if she were physically connected to him, the woman felt a portion of his distress inside herself. An unpleasant tightness started just below her breastbone. For an instant she wondered if in some way this might hurt the baby; then for the first time in months all thoughts of the child went completely out of her mind as she ran for the telephone in the other room.

During the two hours between the telephone call and the arrival of the doctor, the man's distress grew less and less, until half joking, half serious, he suggested that his wife call back and cancel the visit. The return of the running mouse sensation had sent a wave of panic through him. For a minute he had experienced difficulty in breathing and felt flushed and chilled by turns, but as soon as he heard his wife talking to the doctor over the telephone and heard her repeat his words, "Stomach flu . . . it's going around . . ." the breathing distress diminished and the churning and stirring in his abdomen became increasingly tolerable.

"I almost never get sick, except for colds and sinus, that is." The man grinned at the doctor to cover his embarrassment; he somehow felt that calling a physician was a form of weakness unless one was injured or critically ill. "Last time I saw a doctor was in the Army—before they discharge you they give you a check-up," he explained, still feeling awkward and afraid that the other man did not really believe him. "It's been three, almost four years."

"You went to the doctor last year to have your sinuses drained," his wife corrected him.

"Oh, yes, I'm sorry, I forgot." The man squirmed and grinned again. "She has a better memory than me." He tried to hide his annoyance toward his wife by shrugging his shoulder.

"He was stuffed up and I couldn't get any sleep; he kept snoring or sniffing all night. I made him go to the doctor."

The tiny bit of manliness that his wife had threatened was restored when she accepted the blame for his trip to the doctor. "She kept nagging me and complaining about not being able to sleep, so I went." This statement was made in a patronizing tone to let the doctor know that he had indulged his wife in her whim and at the same time to form a bond between himself and the doctor, who no doubt had a wife of his own.

The man might have saved himself the energy of his explanation. The doctor, although looking in his direction and occasionally nodding, was not listening to his patient's words. He was mechanically, out of long practice, evaluating the appearance of the sick man: the skin color, the rate of breathing, condition of the eyes, color of the tongue and a score of other bodily signs—indications as to the severity of the illness and the direction he might have to explore to determine its nature. "Probably some darn bug or other. It's these healthy ones that get most upset when they get sick, can't believe it's happening to them."

The doctor started rubbing his hands together to warm them before he touched the patient's body. "Should have had them come into the office; there'll be a half dozen waiting by the time I get there." He smiled and nodded at his patient. "Better warm these up. You'll go through the ceiling if I touch you without . . . it's cold today. Besides," the doctor used a special jovial tone that he had tested and found particularly effective, "as they say, 'cold hands mean a warm heart'."

He gave his hands several more vigorous rubs, and told himself this was a young couple who would need the services of a family doctor for many years; thus he should look upon this house call as an investment for the future. Momentarily, he turned his attention to the woman, and experienced a tug of resentment. Almost as soon as it arose, he thrust it down

into his subconscious—the woman took her maternity problems to a specialist, routine pregnancies and births were now
the property of obstetricians. The bread and butter of the
old-time general practitioner was gone forever. He was now
left with colds and flus and splinters and simple fractures and
house calls. . . . It took an effort of will to force the resentment back down. As he started examining the patient, one
final bit of irritation slipped out of its hiding place. "Half my
cases are hypochondriacs," he muttered to himself.

"It's some kind of flu." The doctor pulled his prescription pad out of his breast pocket and readied his pen. "I can
give you a prescription to settle your stomach, but," he laid
his pen down for a moment, "if you can avoid taking drugs,
you're better off." The doctor turned to the woman. "If he
starts vomiting, call me and I'll call the drugstore. But if he
hasn't thrown up by now, I think we don't have anything to
worry about."

"It feels like there's something running around inside."
The man chuckled; he had been careful to avoid describing
his symptoms this way during the course of the examination.
He had defined them as "a funny sensation, a tickling." Now
just to make doubly sure that nothing important had been
missed by the doctor, he laughingly referred to his distress as
a mouse running around inside his abdomen.

"You better speak to your wife about her cooking," the
doctor guffawed. "Or—," he hesitated, assessing in his mind
the sophistication of his patient, "maybe you have a case of
'pregnantitis sympathectic.'" The couple started laughing;
they both knew what was expected of them. The doctor,
pleased with himself, unconsciously rubbed his now warm
hands several additional times.

"Give him lots of juice, lots of liquids, soft drinks, cola,
lime cola, slime cola," he guffawed again. The doctor had
given the exact same prescription a thousand times. Each time

he laughed and expected his patients to laugh. He was not disappointed. The couple dutifully laughed a second time and as a gesture of comradeliness, the sick man repeated the doctor's words.

"Slime cola. Don't forget, honey. And remember what the doctor said, watch that cooking. No more mice in the stew."

Two hours later the woman called the doctor and told him in a frantic voice that her husband was vomiting blood.

# 3

The sound of the siren was not as loud inside the ambulance as the man had expected. When they carried him out of his house on a stretcher, he had wondered if the noise would be greater than he could stand. All the noises in his house—the sound of the ambulance attendant's footsteps, his wife's voice, his own breathing—all these sounds had distressed him.

He had fainted after he stopped vomiting. He'd noticed the blood coming out and was surprised—not upset, just surprised—and called his wife's attention to it more as a matter of curiosity than anything else. She took one look and ran for the telephone. He remembered that he'd thought it rather strange that his wife reacted so strongly. The whole regurgitation process had relieved him and his insides felt settled, so he threw off the covers and started to get out of bed. As he remembered it, he'd wanted to tell his wife not to be worried and not to bother the doctor. The next thing he knew he was lying on the floor and his wife was scrubbing his face with a cold, wet towel. Part of the towel she used as a rag, part as a fan. He remembered how unpleasant the cold towel felt on his face and how irritating he found his wife's crying. Her sounds went through his head and seemed to push on the backs of his eyeballs.

"I thought the siren would be so loud inside the ambulance that my head would explode. Funny, it just sounds like a baby crying, not at all like I expected." The sick man looked up at his wife. She sat pressed against his stretcher inside the speeding vehicle. He waited for her reaction, but she acted as if she hadn't heard him. "I expected my head to burst, I couldn't stand the idea of all that noise." His wife still didn't respond. Then he realized that he hadn't been speaking at all. It felt like speech but had only been movements inside his throat.

The white-coated attendant leaned over and adjusted the oxygen mask covering the sick man's mouth and nose. "Just take it easy, sport. Just breathe nice and deep. There's nothing for you to worry about." He patted the patient's arm, then with the same hand checked the restraining straps that held the man secure on the stretcher.

"What do you think is the matter with him?" The woman tugged at the attendant's sleeve bringing his ear close to her lips. "Yesterday he was fine and today—all that blood."

"I don't know what's the matter with him, lady. I'm no doctor. Probably a bleeding ulcer. They always look much worse than they are when an ulcer pops. Soon as they get some blood into him, he'll be OK."

"An ulcer? Is that what you think he has?"

"How should I know? I'm only an ambulance attendant. It's not for me to make any diagnosis." He shook his head to add emphasis to his words. "When we get to the hospital, the admitting doctor will look him over and may come up with a diagnosis."

The attendant dropped his voice several notches, almost but not quite to the point where his words would be drowned out by the wail of the siren. "I'm not allowed to make any statement about a patient's illness. We're not supposed to know anything. Some kid fresh out of medical school with

15

the ink still wet on his diploma can write down anything he pleases. He can say you got leprosy or the plague or St. Vitus Dance and the others will take him serious, but a nurse that's been at it twenty years or an ambulance attendant that has made maybe three thousand pick-ups—we ain't allowed to speak about a patient's illness." The attendant softened his voice and continued to himself. "If you even hint at at diagnosis to some of these sons o' bitches, if you're as sure . . . if you even try to suggest as polite as you can . . . the jerks. Some of them think their shit don't stink just because their daddies could put them through medical school." The attendant looked at the woman out of the corner of his eye to see if she had heard the first part of his statement. Now that the words were out, he felt uneasy and was sorry he had spoken.

The woman's eyes were opened wide, wider than was normal, and although focused in his direction they appeared to be staring at some point far away in the distance. "She didn't hear a word," the attendant whispered, watching the woman's face to see if she noticed the movement of his lips. "She's out on her feet. Be lucky if I don't end up this trip with two patients instead of one." He shifted his attention back to the sick man. "I'd bet a week's pay he's got a bleeding ulcer, but they'll fuss and fuss before they finally decide. It's all a matter of chance."

A thought that had come to the attendant many times in the past formed again. Bits of this thought were always with him and these bits had a tendency to coalesce during trips in the ambulance. "If most people realized how much chance there is, they wouldn't be able to sleep at night. Some live and they don't even know how lucky they are, and yet if things were even a little different—boom, they would be dead. If this guy didn't have a wife, he mighta' lain there in his blood and vomit and died without anyone knowing." The attendant increased the flow of oxygen a little and winked at the prone man who appeared to be looking at him. "There's been times if I had been five minutes earlier . . . or five minutes later . . . it's all one big chance like dealing blackjack."

The sick man saw the attendant's wink and wondered what he meant by it. "He knows I'm not really all that sick. They're making a great big fuss for nothing. He gets paid so what does he care—let them have their fun. Except for that tingling in my fingers and toes, I feel lots better than I did before. I was so worried I wouldn't be able to stand the noise of the ambulance. It just goes to show—I'm going to remember it for the future—you worry about things and then when they happen it's not so terrible at all." He allowed his eyes to flutter closed and experienced the vibration of the vehicle as it maneuvered in and out of traffic. His mind felt like a dish of half-solidified jello, responsive to any vibration, quivering, ready to spill over in any direction if suddenly jolted. It was a different but not unpleasant state of being. "Like how I used to worry about how I'd feel if they ever took me away in an ambulance. I remember thinking about it every night for weeks after they took the guy upstairs away." His jello mind vibrated back to the scene until it felt, rather than remembered, what happened.

The man who lived upstairs. He had lived there for eighteen years, Mr. Tannenbaum, an old Jew who had escaped from the Nazis. The ambulance woke everyone on the block. It was just growing light outside, but it was too early for people to be up. The attendants carried Mr. Tannenbaum out of the building. He was tightly strapped to the stretcher; his face looked like greasy butcher's paper. They shoved him into the vehicle like a nickel into a slot and drove off with the noise of the siren rattling the house windows.

"I used to worry about being put into one of these things as if that meant I'd never come back. I must have thought about it hundreds of times—like an ambulance was a moving

17

coffin and once you were in, that was the end." He turned his head toward his wife as far as he was able and tried to catch her eye. He nodded several times and was delighted when she shifted position and returned his glance. He wanted her to know that he wasn't upset at riding in an ambulance; that he was not like Tannenbaum; that he would be taking the ride back home. He tried to tell her these things and was surprised when she failed to smile and nod her understanding. Then he remembered the oxygen mask. A moment later he forgot about his wife as his mind slipped off to explore another corner of his memory.

"All this excitement." The woman tentatively touched her abdomen. "I better be careful. It's enough that he's sick without taking a chance with the baby." As if the thought had hidden within it a bit of substance, substance sharp as a needle, the woman felt a stab. She pressed her belly with both hands to see whether the pain was from a kick or, if not . . . The second jab calmed her; she felt the movement. "What a healthy little monster." Her tense mouth softened into a near smile. "Nothing bothers this one." The smile formed for a moment as her protecting hands felt a series of little kicks. "No need to waste my energy worrying about the baby." The thought was scarcely formed when she felt a wave of guilt sweep through her. She shifted halfway around and, leaning over her husband, made a series of unnecessary adjustments to his blanket. Then she put her face close to his; but his eyes were far away. They were swimming in memories and could not see her.

"He's been under an awful lot of pressure. He was dragging around all week and he wouldn't stay home. He didn't want to lose a single day's pay. It must be hard being a man—all that responsibility. A woman can stay home and watch her stomach grow and feel all those things happening inside of her; but a man, he's got to go to work regardless of how he feels so that there's enough money." Without her being aware of what was happening, the woman's thoughts turned into whispered words.

"I used to think that men were luckier than women, that they could do what they wanted and had more fun. I guess I didn't know. You have to work and work and worry, and we get to have babies. We have them all to ourselves, inside, for months and months, while you have to make sure not to lose a day's work."

She looked carefully to see if her husband had heard her, then continued speaking to the unaware man in the same fashion she had spoken many times to the unaware baby inside her. "I know everything will be all right. You're not as sick as you look. It's just that when you lose a lot of blood, you look peculiar. I bet you'll live for at least another half century. You don't have to worry about a thing when you come home in a day or two. I'll cook you a bunch of nice dishes and you can watch whatever programs you want on the TV. You usually look so big and healthy. It's easy to forget that you're not a machine. I'm not worried a bit, not a tiny little bit." She held her thumb and forefinger in a measuring position before the unseeing eyes. "A couple of days in the hospital and then maybe a week at home in bed . . . we can take a loan from the bank for the baby. I'm not worried one single . . ." Before she was able to complete the sentence, the woman burst into tears and pressed her face down into the blanket covering her unconscious husband.

# 4

Pressed against one wall of the long hospital corridor were three wooden benches reserved for relatives of emergency admissions. They were placed in a tight row just inside the double doors. At times when the doors opened inward under the pressure of a vigorously pushed gurney, the edge of one door would strike the corner of the first bench. Several inches of wood had been chipped off in this fashion. The location of the benches and the fact that they were the only items of furniture in the long, harshly lit corridor told their purpose far better than the faded hand-lettered sign suspended from a capped gas pipe near the ceiling.

The excitement of the ambulance ride had left the woman feeling dizzy. She sat at the end of the bench closest to the door, holding her head in her hands. The benches had been fully occupied when she came in, but her appearance caused a ripple of activity among the occupants, and a space—albeit the least desirable—was produced. She lifted her head a moment and looked down the hallway. It appeared to extend for a distance of half a city block. Somewhere down that corridor her husband's gurney had disappeared. She had strained to follow its progress, but the dazzle of the lights on the dead white tiles made things indistinct at the far end of the hall.

The presence of the other people sitting on the benches made it easier for her to wait at the entrance and allow her husband to be taken away. This was the rule. There was no choice—she had to wait. It never occurred to the woman to question the validity of the rule or to demand an exception, nor had it occurred to any of the other waiting people.

For several minutes she kept her head in her hands, resting her eyes, allowing her thoughts to drift without any attempt to control them. The intense brightness of the lights left her with whirls of red and orange and spheres of purple and blue behind her closed eyelids. The colors were like the tasseled hats that children wore when she was little. They bobbed up and down on the children's heads and were reflected against the white brilliance of the snow. She remembered the line of children entering the big building through double swinging doors and how her mother stopped just inside the door while all the children continued down the long grey corridor.

The woman smiled, keeping her eyelids closed. She still saw the children shuffling away down that other hallway while she now waited next to swinging double doors.

"Your husband?" A fat, middle-aged woman with cigarette breath and small brownish teeth asked the question. Accepting the other's silence as confirmation, the fat woman continued, "You get used to it. I've had mine here five times. Do you think they know what's wrong with him? First they thought maybe a heart attack, then they were looking for an ulcer. Each time they try out a new theory. I'm convinced it's mental. He thinks the wrong thoughts and gets aggravated and he gets sick. Look at me," the fat woman lifted her arms in an expressive gesture, "I eat too much, I drink more than is good for me, I smoke—everything. And I haven't had a sick day in my life. Take it from me, most of our troubles come from how we think. Some of us are out to kill ourselves one

21

way or another. With my husband, he aggravates, that's the fast way. With me, it's bad habits, that's the slow way. Don't worry, I know my day is coming too, but with my attitude I don't give a damn. I still got some time to wait."

The torrent of words confused the younger woman. The harsh breath and strident chuckly voice made her uncomfortable. She would have liked to return to the colors and memories, but felt obliged to respond with a show of politeness which only served to encourage the other.

"It's possible he might not make it this time." The older woman began to examine the space between her gums and lips with the tip of her tongue. "If he doesn't," her tongue movements caused her words to come out thick, "I'll miss him, but I won't let it break me up. When you come down to it, you're alone in this world and you got to be ready to go it by yourself. I'm not gonna let his thing drag me down too. I'm not going to let anybody or anything cut into my life. You don't do them any good and all you end up is being sick or dead yourself."

"If he," the younger woman started choking up with crying, "if he should die, I'd, I'd die too. I couldn't go on another day, not without . . ." She looked in the direction they had taken her husband and started sobbing.

"That's what you think now. He's not going to die," the fat woman softened her statement with this reassurance. "Twenty, thirty, forty years from now, that's another question, but don't you believe you can't live without him or without anyone."

"I wouldn't want to go on living." The young woman still sobbed, but her hard crying was over.

"Don't you believe it. I love my husband too. Maybe I love him more than a lot of women. I don't want to see him die. I don't want to see anyone die. I think death stinks. But the only one it would really kill me to see die is me. And I'll tell you another thing. There's nobody in this whole big wide world about to die if I kick off or if the most beautiful girl on earth kicks off. When you go, you go alone!"

"But what about my baby?"

"What about your baby?" The older woman didn't understand for a moment what the other meant.

"If I should die, it would die too." Fresh sobs started to form as the young woman began to think about the helpless infant inside her body.

"This whole damn conversation is silly." The fat woman snapped her head with annoyance, transferring, in some mysterious fashion, blame for what had been said onto her new acquaintance. "All this talk of death. Your husband isn't going to die and I doubt if mine will either, so let's change the subject."

A hundred feet away, separated from the people on the benches by three thicknesses of brick wall, the young woman's husband lay on a padded metal table, struggling to stay alive. A breathing tube was stuck in an opening in the man's throat and an oversized transfusion needle protruded from the crook of each arm. Several electrodes attached to the chest, arm and leg of the patient were picking up heartbeat impulses and relaying them to a cardiograph monitored by a flushed, puffy-eyed intern. The intern wore a crumpled white hospital uniform that displayed part of a stethoscope from the jacket pocket. A second doctor—whose attitude toward the intern was such that no one could doubt for a moment that he was a senior resident—was examining the patient, while an angular purse-mouthed nurse made adjustments to the breathing device and transfusion equipment.

"What do you think?" The intern deferred to his senior.

"It's hard to tell without a history. No point guessing. He looks like he's coming around."

"Do you want me to have them send in his wife?" The

23

nurse nodded toward the senior man. "She's waiting out in the corridor. The ambulance attendant said she's very pregnant."

"Did you ever know anyone to be a little bit pregnant?" the senior resident mumbled while he continued to examine the patient.

"Better wait a little while," the intern answered the nurse's question. "If she sees him like this, she might go into labor or faint or something. Let's get some more blood into him and warm him up a little. His signs are still pretty depressed."

"I don't think he would have lasted another ten minutes." The older doctor started to tap his index finger on the chest of the unconscious man. "The lungs sound pretty good, a little liver and spleen enlargement. How's his heart doing?"

"I don't see any damage—essentially normal considering his condition." The intern turned away from the machine and put his stethoscope to the patient's chest. "It's fast, but it's growing stronger. He's coming around. I personally don't think he lost too much blood. He's not hemorrhaging any more. If we can get a good history on him—it's hard to tell without a history." The younger doctor repeated his colleague's statement verbatim.

"I've seen cases like this come in and you wouldn't give a dime for their chances." The resident stopped his examination and yawned, stretching his hands over his head. "They're carried in grey as death and they walk out the next week and with some you never really know what the hell was the matter."

The nurse pursed her mouth as she listened to the doctors talk. She had been wearing her cap for fifteen years. There were times she found herself growing irritated when young doctors, who were still in junior high school when she was already a registered nurse, spoke in an all-knowing superior fashion. There were times she reacted as if the superiority were directed toward her, even though usually this was not the case. "I better get his wife," she announced in a tone that was difficult to contradict. "There are others waiting. This isn't a private sanitarium. We have an obligation to the public, not only to one patient, doctor." Her use of the singular word doctor when two were present made it awkward for either man to respond. Besides, beneath their clinical bravado, they—like almost all other newly hatched doctors—were really a little afraid of getting into arguments with the old-time nurses. If word got up to the hospital administrator that an intern or resident was unable to get along with the nursing staff, one's entire career might be affected.

Hearing no contradiction to her announced intention, the nurse wheeled around and walked out into the corridor. The two doctors caught each other's eyes for a moment and exchanged a look that covered their feelings of helpless irritation; a look of 'we have to humor the old bitch,' when each would have much preferred to kick her in the ass.

25

# 5

The swollen hospital squatted like an ugly giant toad on the top of a hill in the old section of the city. Like a toad's crooked arms and legs, extensions had grown out of the body of the structure, zig-zagging halfway down both sides of the hill. The older portions of the hospital had darkened from their original bright brick magenta to the brownish red of dried blood. It was as if the hundreds and thousands of suffering people who had lain in the wards and rooms of the old buildings had, with their wounds, saturated the very walls. The newer portions were of a variety of colors: grey and green wooden buildings built twenty-five years earlier as a temporary expediency to handle the burgeoning population, tan prefabricated structures added in the last ten years to house student nurses and interns, and a sparkling new cream-colored building, built with special government research money, containing lavishly equipped laboratories and ultra-modern facilities for fifty patients—patients specially selected because of their suitability as teaching subjects.

Connecting the various buildings was a maze of passageways constructed of brick or corrugated iron, and lined on the inside with either white tile or light green squares of fiberboard.

Only one building stood apart from the rest. It was a

concrete block structure containing boilers and electrical generators. Its basement housed the morgue and autopsy rooms. Though apparently unconnected to the rest of the complex when viewed from the outside, this building was joined to the others by several underground passageways whose entrance doors were kept locked at all times.

The hospital, although it was located in and served the needs of one of the more densely populated parts of the city, was quite isolated from the city. It was a community almost entire unto itself and could be likened to one of the independent cities that studded Europe during the late Middle Ages. Like the old cities, the hospital demanded absolute obedience to all its rules and proclamations—rules and proclamations developed by the rulers alone, not subject to the vote or veto of the inhabitants; rules that were often different from and at times contrary to the laws and customs of the outside community.

Those who ran the hospital had almost complete authority to designate who might enter or leave. As in the old European cities, many people were forced to seek refuge inside the hospital walls, refuge from the attacks of dangerous enemies. Others entered to earn a living, or to practice their calling, or to seek an education.

The hospital, although equipped with the gadgets and knowledge of the twentieth century, was in fact a dukedom or barony with the philosophy and political character of the fifteenth. Absolute belief in the infallibility of the ruling class was demanded of all who entered. Only among the rulers— those whose power was attested to by the rigid use of their title of nobility—only among the doctors themselves was any disagreement or questioning permitted.

The classes of the hospital inhabitants were identifiable by their clothing. Attending physicians, whose right to use the hospital was granted subject to good behavior, were permitted to wear the clothing of the outside, except when they entered special places given over to the rites of surgery. Then they were required to dress in green. The house physicians were clothed in white as were the nurses. Higher nurses wore caps; lesser nonregistered nurses went bareheaded. Matrons and orderlies were dressed in light blue. Janitors wore dark grey, food service workers light grey. Medical students wore white jackets, and to distinguish themselves from ward clerks and social workers they, to a man, dangled stethoscopes from their pockets.

The lowest class, the class with the fewest rights, certainly with no right of privacy and no right to share in decisions affecting their own fate, was the patients. They were the serfs of the hospital dukedom, wholly dependent upon the other classes, expected to respond with slavish obedience, often denied knowledge about what was being done to their bodies or about the seriousness of their condition. It was considered perfectly proper to lie to them, to reassure them even when they hovered at the brink of death. Radical procedures of questionable effectiveness might be applied to them without their being made aware of the possible consequences. They were individuals to whom the right to die, though they be hopelessly ill and broken with pain, was absolutely denied. This class also was dressed in its own special clothing: bedclothes that tied in the rear making modesty difficult for the patient who had full control of his faculties and impossible for all the rest.

More than any other reason, the hospital existed as an independent isolated community with its own laws, customs and philosophy because the rest of the city shunned it. The tens of thousands of people who lived beneath its widespread shadow knew of its existence—in some tiny corner of their minds most had exact knowledge of its location, of the fastest route of reaching its gate—but the hospital was a place to be shunned, a place to which the diseased were sent, a place where people went to die.

Hanging over the hospital, mixed with the haze and fog that hovered about its jumbled structure, oozing through its wards, corridors and subterranean passageways, was an invisible unmeasurable substance compounded of equal parts pain and anger. The people of the city were afraid of the concentrated anger stuffed into the hospital; they stayed away and tried not to think about the place, and were glad for its thick walls, its gates and isolation.

Of all the places in the city, the one never visited by the afternoon stroller, by the bored housewife or the vacationing student, was the hospital. Even the local cemetery had its share of visitors, those who found peace enjoying the lush green of carefully tended lawns; even the skid row with its rag bundle human beings lying like neglected garbage in urine-drenched hallways was visited by sightseers and slummers. But the hospital was never visited for pleasure.

# 6

The woman did not faint or go into labor when she saw her husband lying on the table in the emergency examining room. She was surprised at his appearance but not shocked or frightened. The profusion of equipment affixed to his body made her feel that he was now safe, that he was in the hands of experts. She had complete faith in the ability of the doctors and in the facilities of the hospital. The tubes, needles and wires attached to her husband reassured her. He was being cared for; there was no more need to worry; nothing could happen now. She sat down and was able to take in deep breaths of air; for hours she had been breathing in shallow rapid gasps, tiny bites of air that filled the upper part of her chest but were not satisfying. The deep breaths made her tingle; they relaxed and satisfied her and caused her to grow a little sleepy.

"Your husband had a close call." The resident sat down next to the woman with a pad of hospital record paper on his knee. "He's much better now, but we want to keep him under close observation for the next twenty-four to forty-eight hours."

The woman scarcely heard the doctor's words. She was enjoying the feeling of her deep breathing and the warm syrupy sensation that was filling her body. She smiled and nodded her head.

The doctor hesitated, puzzled for a moment at the woman's smile. Then in a louder tone, "Did you hear me, are you all right?"

"I'm fine. I'm fine. It's just that this is the first time I've had a chance to relax in hours. Now that I know he's safe, I feel like I want to lie down somewhere and go to sleep. My bones feel like they're made of putty."

"He's better, much better than when he came in, but I didn't say that he was safe." The resident chose his words carefully. He did not want to alarm the woman, but he did want her to know that her husband's condition was still very serious. He believed that relatives should always be made aware of the chance of a sudden catastrophe if that possibility existed. He did not subscribe to the theory that relatives should be kept in ignorance. He had known of too many cases where a husband or wife or parent had left the hospital believing everything was all right, that the patient was out of danger. He had witnessed and on occasion had been the subject of their reaction when the patient suddenly died: bewilderment followed by anger at the doctor for not telling them there was a chance of death, anger at not being allowed to worry—at being allowed to enjoy some hours of peace while their loved one was suffering and dying. There were cases enough when death did come unexpectedly to plague the hospital staff. The resident had no hesitancy in warning relatives of danger. With patients it was different. A dead patient could not accuse you of not telling him; besides it was easier to manage a case when the patient believed everything would be all right. It upset the staff when a patient knew he was terminal and talked about it or cried out for a kind of comfort that no one could provide.

"Your husband is much better, his blood pressure is

31

almost back to normal and he is breathing easier, but we cannot predict at this point the course of his illness. We don't want to needlessly worry you, but at the same time we don't want you to leave here thinking that there isn't a chance of a sudden, ah—," the resident hesitated, groping for a suitable expression, "of a sudden turn for the worse."

The woman forced herself to listen to the doctor's words. She understood them and nodded several times to let him know that she was paying close attention, but she did not feel what he was saying. The complex equipment and the presence of two doctors and a nurse in their white uniforms were proof against any disaster. She nodded her head as she had on hundreds of occasions when her father warned her about being careful when she crossed the street. She had nodded her head, but her father's words, like the words of the resident, meant nothing to her. Getting hit by a car was something that could not happen to her. It was perfectly proper for her parent to warn her; someday she would warn her own children; but the danger was not real. There were no speeding automobiles in her parents' living room, just as there was no danger with two doctors, a nurse and dozens of pieces of complicated equipment taking care of her husband. The resident was giving her a perfectly proper father-type warning and the woman listened and nodded and forced her face to frown seriously, but she did not believe a word. Even telling the doctor about her husband's symptoms and describing the onset of his illness did not cause her any discomfort; and she quickly signed the release forms the nurse handed her, without reading them or asking a single question about their meaning.

The man stared up at the circular neon light attached to the ceiling. Alongside the dazzling white tube was an old unused fixture with six empty sockets. "I wonder if you'd get a shock if you put your finger in one of them?" The man's thoughts drifted away from the fixture and across the white ceiling. "Funny how everything is white, the light is white, the ceiling is white, the walls are white—I wonder if I'm white?" He did not want to make the effort of looking at himself. Besides it wasn't important. "I feel white." The thought like a wisp of white cloud drifted over his mind. "Do you feel black when you're dead?" he asked himself. "I must be OK 'cause I feel so damn white—I wish that damn light wasn't so damn bright." He enjoyed the damns and decided to shout out a few damns. They would make him feel better. The words were there in his brain and he shaped them with his lips and tongue, but nothing would come out. Then he noticed the breathing tube stuck into an opening in his throat. It felt like a cold sore throat. He hadn't noticed it before. He wondered why, then forgot about it. It was there so it was supposed to be there. That was enough for him. "I wonder what happened to the ambulance?" He vaguely remembered the ambulance, something that had happened a long time ago, or was it just a little while? It was hard to remember. He wondered if his wife was still in the ambulance. Then he let the thought slip away. He looked back at the empty sockets in the unused ceiling fixture. "They're girls and bulbs are boys." A chuckle ran up the inside of his chest. "You screw a bulb into a socket and when it gets all the way in, it lights up." He was delighted with his new idea. "That's why they put up that neon tube. The other was too dirty. They don't want dirty things going on in the hospital." He knew he was in the hospital, but didn't know how he knew. "Mustn't get the patients too excited, bad for their blood pressure." He was fascinated with the empty sockets and decided to stick his finger into one of them to see what would happen. He tried to lift his arm, but it wouldn't move; the effort sent a wave of aching through the limb and was exhausting. He closed his eyes and then was able to climb out of his body and reach up to the ceiling. He thrust each of his hands into sockets that

33

had grown large and deep and pushed his arms up and up until suddenly a tremendous shock of current tore down both arms into his chest, through his guts and groin and down into his legs.

A gasping, groaning sound came out of the patient's mouth; his eyes were wide open and filmed with agony. The blood and oxygen finally had brought him back to full consciousness and the terrible ache in his legs and arms and the rodent racing in his belly hit his brain like jets of live steam.

"Are you having much pain?" The intern was the first to notice the patient's return to consciousness and his distorted facial expression. "We'll give you something to make you feel better, something to put you to sleep, but if you can hold on for a few minutes, I need to ask you some questions." The resident interrupted the history he was taking from the patient's wife, but did not attempt to interfere with his younger colleague. The intern placed the fingertips of his left hand on the sick man's wrist. The young doctor's puffy eyes had grown noticeably more swollen and both of his cheeks were mottled with a high red which extended to his ears. His face was almost entirely free of expression. The only message his features communicated was that of deep weariness. As was the lot of all interns, he had scarcely known a night of uninterrupted sleep since starting his service; he felt as if a long needle were lodged in his head just behind his eyeballs.

"I'm going to take out the breathing tube and let you breathe on your own." The intern shifted his glance for a moment to the resident who answered the look with a tiny affirmative head movement. "Just breathe nice and easy and don't get upset if you have some trouble catching your breath for a few seconds." The doctor completed his adjustments with the help of the nurse, then gave the patient's wrist a slight squeeze to let him know that he had cooperated satisfactorily. "Don't try and talk loud. Whisper, I can hear, and rest if you get too tired. Now, try and describe how you feel."

The sick man opened his mouth and for half a minute could only make a croaking noise. Then gaining command of his throat muscles and regulating his breathing, he whispered, "My throat is burning. Feels like I swallowed boiling coffee."

"That's from the work we did on you. You were pretty sick when they brought you in. Tell us what else you feel?"

"I feel very bad, doctor." As he whispered the words the man wanted to cry. He wanted to cry more than anything else in the world, but he couldn't. "Boys don't cry; girls cry." His father's words, first spoken more than twenty years earlier, held the sobs silent inside his chest. His eyes filled with tears, but the sobs would not come. "I feel sick all over. Never felt like this before."

"Exactly how do you feel? What's hurting you?"

"My arms, my legs, they ache, they feel as if someone hit them with a baseball bat. Hit them a hundred times each. And my back, it hurts too, and my head, everything." The sick man stopped speaking and spent several minutes catching his breath while he recovered from the exertion. During this time the intern remained silent and indicated by an impatient shake of his head that the nurse should stay where she was and not make any adjustments to the transfusion equipment or electrodes.

With a deep prolonged sigh the man continued. "The ache isn't so bad right now. It went away a little, but my arms and legs feel so funny, like someone shoved ice inside the bones, not the skin or flesh, the bones. It feels like all my bones are frozen solid."

The intern looked back at the resident who had been straining to catch every word. The younger doctor had a questioning expression on his face and he held the other's glance for several seconds until the resident answered the un-spoken question with a slight shrug of his shoulders.

"Anything else you can tell us about how you feel? Any place in particular that feels worse than the rest?"

"I thought it stopped, but now it started again." The patient's eyes began to shift laterally back and forth as an attack of acute panic seized him. "My belly," he gasped, pulling against the restraining straps that held him to the table. "I've got a mouse running crazy inside my belly. Take it out, take it out, doctor, please. Cut me open and take out the little bastard. I can't stand it any more. Cut me open, cut me open—it's tearing my guts to pieces."

The intern nodded to the nurse who quickly jabbed a syringe into the patient's arm. She pressed the plunger down with a carefully controlled movement and by the time the hypodermic was empty, the sick man had grown quiet except for an occasional soft moan that issued from his wide open mouth.

The patient's wife had not moved and had not spoken during the period of her husband's consciousness. She listened to every word and although seated had strained to watch his movements. It never entered her mind that she might have the right to speak to her husband or to comfort him. When it became apparent that the sick man had succumbed to the sedation, the woman stood up and approached him cautiously. Had any of the other three so much as frowned, she would have returned to her seat, but there was no opposition. She leaned over the man and looked at his face. His mouth gaped wide and his skin had lost its flush. It was the color of boiled fish. He looked unfamiliar—twenty years older than the man she had lived with. He looked old and tired and sick. "He's very sick, isn't he, doctor?" The woman turned to the resident who had resumed physical examination of the patient and was probing the upper abdomen. "Do you know what's wrong with him?"

The resident shook his head without interrupting the

36

examination. "We can only guess at this point." He did not look up at the woman who spoke. "I told you before that he was a pretty sick boy, but I think he's safe for now. We'll run a series of tests on him. As soon as we find out exactly what's wrong, we'll do whatever is necessary to help him get well."

The woman inclined her head. "I thought once he was in the hospital, you would know what was wrong. I thought you could give him some medicine or something."

"Lady," the resident allowed a trace of irritation to harshen his voice, "doctors are not miracle workers. We're examining your husband; he will be given a number of diagnostic tests and procedures. Then we will evaluate all our findings and arrive at a diagnosis. In the meantime I suggest that you go home and get some rest. If we need you, we'll call you."

The woman hesitated several moments, wondering if the doctor meant that she would have to leave. Her question was answered by the nurse. "If we need you, we'll call. If you insist on waiting, you can sit out in the lobby." With the movements of a sergeant who expects to be obeyed, the nurse opened the examining room door and ushered the woman out.

Without thinking about what she was doing, the woman walked down the hallway, stopping in front of the occupied benches. She had not been offended by the resident or the nurse. They were in charge. They knew the rules. Besides, she didn't feel as if the sick man belonged to her. He belonged to the hospital. He didn't even look like her husband. When they made him well, she would take him back. Until then, she had signed him over to the doctors and nurses in the hospital. He was their worry. The woman sat on the bench and felt nothing. She didn't feel good or bad. She was neither worried nor happy. She was blank—almost as if she had had her brain anesthetized. Even the fatigue that earlier caused her body to sag and her eyes to burn had evaporated.

37

"Well, how is he?" The fat woman stood directly in front of the bench with her hands on her hips. "Did they tell you what's wrong?"

The seated woman shook her head and mumbled, "They said they have to make tests."

"Tests! That's what they always say when they don't know. Every time my husband has come to this place they make tests. If the doctors knew what they were doing, they wouldn't have to make so damn many tests. Mine isn't so good. He looks worse than the last time. I got a funny feeling right here—," the fat woman pointed to a spot between her swollen breasts. "I got a feeling that he might not make it this time."

The younger woman looked up and allowed her eyes to examine the other's face. It was deep red in color. Layers of fat hid most of the expression so that it was difficult to tell if she were happy or unhappy. "If you talk that way, he will die." The young woman was surprised at her own words. They came out without her planning. "All the bad thoughts get inside and they die."

"Do you really think so?" Wonder filled the older woman's voice.

"Yes. I just figured it out."

"Then how do they get sick in the first place? Do you think it's other people's bad thoughts that make you sick?" The fat woman said the word 'other' with such emphasis that bits of saliva sprayed from her mouth.

"I helped mine to get sick. I really didn't care what was happening to him. I thought about the baby most of the time. With all the bad that's floating around, all it takes is your own bad thoughts added to the rest."

"You are crazy as a bedbug! The idea that I made him sick! You," the fat woman pointed her stubby sausage finger at the other, "are nutty as a jaybird. I knew I shouldn't have wasted my time talking to you!"

38

The young woman dropped her head and stared down at her lap. She didn't care what the other said. She knew she was right and that was enough.

"It was my husband's negative thoughts that made him sick. Your own bad thoughts are what make you sick. Nobody else. You do it to yourself."

"No. I don't think so." The seated woman kept her eyes lowered and spoke in a soft but very certain voice. "It's not like you say. It's not only what we do to ourselves. Maybe that's a part of it. I can't argue there, but mostly it's what we do to each other. We kill each other. Not only wives and husbands, but parents and friends. Yes," the woman looked up at the angry, fleshy face above her, "and strangers too. It all adds up together—everything."

"You are a rude little snip. If I were your mother I'd slap your face." With that the fat woman angrily shoved through the double doors and stood snorting in the frosty air outside muttering, "If she weren't pregnant, I'd have slapped her face myself."

# 7

The woman remained seated on the bench. She folded her arms over her distended abdomen and allowed her eyes to close, though her mind felt fresh and wide awake. "I was right," she whispered to herself. "I didn't want to see it before now." She sighed the way her grandmother had sighed after her grandfather died. The old woman would look at her dead husband's picture and murmur, "If I could only have him back, for a day even. For an hour. There are so many things I never told him. Arguments, arguments, and now he's gone." The young woman sighed. She felt the pain her old grandmother knew. "There are so many things I never told him." She repeated the old woman's words as her own.

As she sat there with her grandmother's sadness, the woman's thoughts moved back to a time before she was married, to the four years that lay between her graduation from high school and her marriage. It was a period of her life about which she rarely allowed herself to think—a time that had ended only a year and a half earlier, but felt very long ago. One by one her friends became engaged and then married. It started during the last year of high school, reaching its peak a year after graduation. She had attended dozens of showers, dozens of engagement parties and weddings. It seemed like hundreds. Each one was more painful than the one before. Each time she swore that she would refuse the next, would plead sickness or go out of town, but she never did. After two years of weddings, over half of her friends were married. Some already had babies. A heavy desperate pressure had crept over her. She didn't have the excuse of college or a career. She would examine herself in the mirror and compare her looks with those of the lucky ones. At night with her door locked she stood before her full-length mirror examining her naked body, telling herself over and over that she had a better figure than this one or that, allowing herself to fantasize the reactions of various young men if they could see her unclothed body. Weeks would pass without any dates, then a rush of activity, then nothing. Sitting at home waiting for the telephone to ring, pretending it didn't really matter. Going out on Saturday with other lonely desperate girls. She did not fight the memories. They sent a dull pain through her skull, but she would not push them away.

The woman started to probe her distended abdomen, but just before her hands touched the drum-hard area she forced them down so that they dangled almost to the floor. "I'm not going to think about the baby until he comes home." She determined on this penance, half knowing as she made the resolve that she wouldn't be able to carry it through.

She remembered the horror of hearing about the pregnancy of one of her classmates. The girl was unmarried, and all anyone could talk about was the illegitimate unborn child. Her mother had asked her about the unfortunate girl. "I hope this is a lesson to you about what can happen. Her poor parents. What a terrible thing to happen to them."

Her mother's words still sounded in her ears. They had been with her every time she went out on a date. After the movie or after the dance as she got into her date's car she would tighten up. She wanted to be kissed and touched, and was upset when nothing happened. She always carried a pack of gum in case it was her breath. But no matter how strongly she felt—at times it had been torture—she would stop her date when he tried to maneuver his hand between her legs. "If they ever touch me there," she told herself, "I won't be able to stop."

Her husband was the first man she allowed to put his hand up her dress. She had dated him a number of times and was pleased that he kept calling. Several months had passed without a lonely Saturday night. She liked him and enjoyed his deep kissing and the sensation of having her breasts caressed. She even permitted him to remove her brassiere and kiss her nipples. She had been startled when during the course of one of their necking sessions he gasped, "I love you, I love you," and with a sudden movement forced his hand up between her thighs. She had grabbed for his arm—her action was almost instinctual—and held it with all her might. Instead of fighting back he pressed his lips to her ear and whispered, "Please, please. I love you." She still held on waiting for one more thing. "I want to marry you," he whispered. "I love you." She remembered how she put both arms around his neck and closed her eyes tight letting herself just feel. Several times as she felt the deep, deep ache of him thrusting into her body, she whispered back, "I love you. I really do." She had never allowed herself to doubt that statement during the months of their engagement or any time after their marriage.

As she sat in the hospital corridor waiting to hear about her husband, with his baby kicking inside her womb, for the first time the woman allowed herself to doubt.

# 8

The man opened his eyes and watched in horror as a devil tried to drive a stake through his heart. The devil wearing the devil's uniform of white leaned over him with a mallet in his hand. The man could not see the stake that was being driven down into his chest. He felt no pain, just the pressure as the mallet struck. A second white devil looked into his eye with a light so bright it was painful. As she looked she murmured, "Don't let the tapping upset you. The doctor is taking a bit of marrow from your breast bone with a hollow needle. It's a simple procedure." The man heard the words and pretended to believe them. He even grunted in response; but he knew they were trying to kill him, and he planned to escape the moment no one was looking. The room was filled with all manner of dangerous equipment, things for torture and for killing. The man knew they had taken him away because there was no old fixture with empty sockets on the ceiling. This room was bright and new with a powerful light shining down on him. "Like they use for third degrees," he thought. "I won't tell them anything. I don't care if they kill me."

Another devil who looked like the doctor who had wanted to poison him with slime cola was in the torture room. "Slime cola," the man chuckled. "What a silly thing, as if I were stupid enough to drink it."

"Sip this." The nurse held a cup containing a small quantity of liquid to his lips. The man shook his head and locked his teeth together. "Now, be a good boy and sip this. It's medicine that will make your stomach feel better."

The man wanted to shout out "No!" but was afraid if he did the lady devil would be able to pour the draft down his throat. He shook his head and muttered through his teeth, "No slime cola. You want to kill me."

"What did he say?" The doctor who was tapping the aspiration needle looked up for a moment.

"Something about slime. Slime soda—he thinks we're trying to poison him."

"Here, let me try." The older doctor who was dressed in street clothes took the cup from the nurse. "When I visited him this morning I told him to drink lots of liquids—lime cola, slime cola." He grinned. "It's one of the things I tell my patients. Makes them feel at ease. When he sees me, he'll take the medicine."

The sick man watched the devil who looked like the doctor who had visited him at his home approach with the glass containing the green liquid. He set his jaws and determined not to open his mouth, even if they hit him with the mallet.

"This will make you feel much better," the doctor cooed. "Come on, open up. You know who I am. I wouldn't give you anything that would hurt."

The man watched the doctor's face and the emerald liquid jiggling in the glass cup. A flood of exhaustion spread through his body and the terrible ache returned. "What's the use," he thought. "They've got me. In another minute the other one will be down inside my heart." He relaxed his jaws, and as the rim of the glass touched his lips he opened his mouth and allowed the liquid to trickle in. The touch of the glass to his lips made him feel as he felt years ago. His father would bring

44

a glass of something good into his bedroom when he lay sick. He drank whatever his father brought without questioning and always felt better.

"See?" The doctor was pleased with his ability to manage the sick man. "The old bedside manner still works. He took it like a baby."

As if a distorting celluloid mask had been ripped from the man's eyes, everything in the gleaming hospital room twisted back into focus. He recognized the doctor who had visited his home and smiled his recognition. "Sure is one hell of a case of the flu," he whispered, holding his smile so that the doctor would not take offense and interpret the words as criticism.

"No point in doing things by halves," the other chuckled back. "When you get sick, you want your doctor to earn his fee. Well," the older man prolonged the word and nodded his head several times in a knowing way, "with a healthy young animal like you the recovery is often as dramatic as the onset. I wouldn't be a bit surprised if you were back on your feet within a week." He turned to the resident who was placing a sterile dressing over the breastbone puncture wound. He caught the younger doctor's eye to let him know that this was all still part of the bedside manner and was not to be interpreted as a diagnostic opinion. The resident showed no reaction to his colleague's words and continued working on the patient.

"Do you really think—I'll be OK—within a week?" A swirl of relief tumbled out of the sick man's brain down through all the nerves and fibers of his body.

"Now, now, young fellow, I didn't say you would be ready to run a mile race within a week." The older doctor tapped his lips with his forefinger, a gesture that he had carefully developed upon entering into practice some twenty-five years earlier, a gesture that denoted thoughtful deliberation and was by now habit. "As I said, I would not be a bit surprised if

45

you were on your feet within a week or ten days. But," he lowered his tone to a pious level, "as they say, a doctor can only treat. It is up to a Greater Power to cure."

The sick man looked up and smiled. He had heard part of the other man's statement, but had allowed his mind to wander and was responding to the tone more than to the words.

The resident turned away from the patient and started to remove his surgical gloves. The nurse, who was preparing the aspirated bone marrow for the laboratory, looked up and caught his eye. The resident shook his head slightly, allowing his mouth to curl for a moment into a look of disgust. "The old bluffer." He silently formed the words, then shook his head a second time as he thought, "Why the hell does he have to interfere with the patient? 'Bedside manner!' 'A week to ten days!' If it's what I think it is, this kid may never make it out. It's one thing not to worry a patient and another to tell him he'll be up and about in a week." He muttered under his breath, "I wish there was some way of keeping them out of our hair."

"Doctor," the sick man spoke out as loudly as he could, drawing the attention of both physicians, "may I see my wife? I want to see if she's all right," he lied. He had suddenly experienced a tightening sensation of unreasoned fear. Something about the room at that instant—the movements of the people, the strangeness of the setting—something told him that, although the pain was for the moment dull and bearable, he was a desperately sick man. He tried to control his voice as he spoke; he did not want them to give him another needle and send him down into the hot, dark sleep. "Is my wife outside? May I see her?" He waited, fighting the gathering panic. He felt so terribly alone. He had to have something familiar to hold onto. "Just for a minute," he pleaded.

"Not yet," the resident mumbled, scarcely paying attention

to his words. "We have some X-rays to do. You'll just have to be patient."

"I'll check and see if she's all right." The older doctor patted his patient's shoulder as he started to leave. "When they assign you to a bed, I'm sure they'll let her look in for a minute."

The sick man dug his nails into his palms fighting a rising panic as the older man left, leaving him with two white uniformed strangers, helpless and alone.

# 9

The vast hospital was filled with loneliness. Each bed in the crowded wards contained its lonely occupant. During the day there were hours of relief, but even for those who knew their discharge date was near, night was a lonely, frightening time. For the very sick, for the very old, for the dying there was no relief. Visitors, if they came, spent an awkward few minutes, then were ushered away. The brief visits only served to intensify the loneliness.

A man gets sick and as punishment for his sickness is taken to a strange place where he lies next to strange suffering people and is treated and handled in the most intimate fashion by individuals he does not know.

Everything is strange and unfamiliar in this place to which the sick man is forced to go. There are no pictures on the walls, no carpets on the floors. The furniture is different; the walls are of a different color. Even the air is different—pungent with antiseptic and disease.

At home the man is treated like a man. He is listened to, makes decisions affecting his life, accepts or rejects the suggestions of others. In the hospital he is treated like a child and can decide nothing.

The terrible loneliness of the hospital—little rooms

containing a single occupant—individuals slipping slowly into death. Rarely are the dying comforted. Often they are not told that they must measure their remaining life in hours. Sometimes they are past the point where they can be told anything. Those who can still think, know. Most know that they are dying as they stare at white ceilings or search inside their darkening minds for a bit of memory to grasp. Those who must die, who cannot be saved, especially the old, are shunned whenever possible. No one knows what to say. Death is frightening and upsetting.

The woman screaming out in labor is lonely. Hour after hour the tearing pains move from a place deep inside her back across her abdomen down into the bottom of her womb. As she lies spread-legged on the table, the man who put the child into her body cannot come and comfort her. She lies exposed and helpless before strangers.

Children in cribs or half-size beds gasp and whimper in their loneliness. They clutch a doll or teddy bear, the only familiar thing left to them. Although swollen with pain, stiffened in casts, dry with fever, the children lie alone without their parents. Parents who kissed and dressed the slightest bruise, who held hands and whispered comfort when nightmares broke into sleep, are now denied the sick and dying children.

# 10

The resident walked down the corridor and stuck his head into the emergency examining room. "We've settled on a diagnosis for that fellow who came in this morning."

The intern looked up from some forms he was completing and rubbed his half-closed eyes. "You mean the one with the pregnant wife?"

"Yes. I'm gonna send him over to the new wing. It's a very interesting case."

"Doesn't sound good." The intern stifled a yawn. "Well, at least he'll be given first-class treatment if he's a teaching subject—if he can stand being examined a dozen times a day. I guess I'd rather be over there," the intern stifled another yawn, "than on the wards. The food's better."

"What do you think we found?" The resident was a trifle annoyed at the younger man's apparent lack of interest.

"Let me see the blood work and I'll hazard a guess."

"Smart boy, doctor." The resident spoke in a friendly, but nevertheless patronizing manner. "It's the first case of acute leukemia in an adult we've seen in several months."

"What do you think the course will be?" The intern was pleased that his tentative but unspoken diagnosis had proved correct.

"Very guarded. That hemorrhage worries me. If he starts again, we'll be in trouble. It's an interesting case. The onset was rapid. If we're lucky, we'll bring him to remission. If we're lucky! You know how easily they get infected."

"Does his wife know? I think she's still sitting outside."

"No. Let her have a night's sleep. Tomorrow's time enough. Besides, I want to run a few more tests."

"You gonna tell her yourself?"

"Yes. Sooner or later we'll want to do a post-mortem. Might as well lay the groundwork now. Tell her how important the case is and how what we learn may someday help others and all that jazz."

"Jesus, you are a coldblooded human being."

"Not at all. I'll do everything in my power to keep him going. Nothing I'd like better than to see him go home for a few months. But you know as well as I, it's just a matter of time. When the time comes I want to be able to ask her to sign a p.m. release and have her do it."

"It would be nice—," the intern hesitated, forcing a yawn so as to appear blasé, "nice for his wife, for both of them if he could stay around until the baby is born."

The resident frowned, knitting his brows until they almost touched. "That's a good thought. It would be nice. Well, we'll give it the old college try. About two months, would you say?"

"Yeah, two months," the intern answered half to himself as the resident left the room. "Let's give it all we got."

The intern fumbled with the forms lying on the table then angrily pushed them away. He shoved his chair back and got up. Turning to the instrument cabinet, he glared at the dozens of shiny steel instruments. "We're all a bunch of cold-blooded bastards," he muttered, picking up a round mirror that was attached to a headband. He toyed with this device used to focus light into various body openings, then examined the inside of his throat in it brilliant surface. He stuck his tongue way out, grunting ugh as he saw its thick whitish coating.

"Checking to see if you have leukemia, doctor?" the resident chortled, thrusting his head partway into the room. "It isn't contagious, you know," he continued in a bantering tone. "It's usually your first year medical students that get all the rare fatal diseases. Those few that somehow manage to live until graduation should be as tough as elephant hides."

The intern reddened with anger and embarrassment. His anger was unconcealed as he turned toward his tormentor. "I don't appreciate your sense of humor one single bit, doctor." The word 'doctor' was almost a snarl.

The resident walked into the room, still grinning. "I'm sorry. I was only kidding. I didn't mean any offense." As he spoke, he tentatively stuck out a hand which the other ignored. "I sometimes do the same thing." He dropped his voice to a confidential tone. "We all do. Especially when we see a case like that one, not much younger than we are. In fact, just after I told his wife to go home, just before I stuck my head in the door, I was thinking the same thing." He offered his hand for the second time. "No hard feelings?"

"No hard feelings. I suppose those who are always dealing with disease have a tendency to worry more than the average person." The intern picked up the reflector and casually examined his eyes, pulling the lower lids down as far as they would go.

"Your worst patient is a doctor. When I was an intern, the first six months I was convinced I had tuberculosis. For the last six months it was something new every week." The resident took the reflector from the other man and looked into his own throat. "I doubt if we have much to worry about; only the good die young."

"Yeah," the intern repeated, but in a different tone of voice, carefully enunciating each word, "only the good die young."

# 11

The man lay with his eyes closed as his gurney was pushed through a series of long connecting corridors by a Negro orderly. Every time they shifted direction or stopped for a moment, he asked the orderly where he was being taken. The black man didn't answer. He saw the patient's lips move, but the words had no breath behind them. Had he heard the sick man's question, he would have answered. He enjoyed talking to patients as he wheeled them about the hospital. It helped to pass the time. But he assumed from the closed eyes that this one was unconscious or under sedation, so he hummed a tune and thought about girls.

"Where are you taking me?" The man formed the words as he felt the movement of the rubber-tired vehicle. He was so deeply exhausted he didn't want to open his eyes. During the final series of X-rays he had fallen asleep on the table—a natural sleep, not one brought on by drugs. When they placed him on the gurney, his sleep was broken. He kept his eyes closed hoping to slip back into sleep as soon as the movement came to an end. The thought of opening his eyes to the white glaring lights overhead was painful. "Where are you taking me?" he whispered again as they turned a corner. He didn't expect an answer. He didn't really care. All he wanted was to be taken someplace dark and quiet, someplace that would rest his aching body, someplace where he could sleep until the deep bone-weariness was gone.

The gurney stopped; then with several expert tugs the orderly shifted the man onto a bed. The movement sent throbs of pain deep into his back and he opened his eyes. "You're going first class, man." The orderly adjusted the sides of the bed as he spoke, sides that were raised to prevent helpless or very sick patients from falling out of bed. "Private room, your own private john, in the new part of the hospital You must rate." The sick man smiled weakly. He wanted the other to know his friendliness was appreciated. The orderly smiled back. "Be like having a vacation in your own exclusive hotel room. You sure do rate."

"Thanks," the sick man spoke as loudly as he could, but it was scarcely above a whisper. "Sure do appreciate everything."

"That's OK, mister. No need to thank me. Glad to be of service. I'll come by and see you tomorrow evening, hear?"

The sick man nodded and lifted his hand several inches in a gesture of friendship as the orderly left the room.

During the few minutes it took for the night nurse to make all the necessary adjustments to his equipment, the man kept his eyes closed. He didn't want to speak or be forced to listen. He didn't know what the nurse looked like and didn't care. All he wanted was darkness and silence and sleep.

After the nurse left the room, the man slowly opened his eyes. The light was out and except for the glow from the corridor filtering through the partially opened door, it was dark. He hadn't moved or tried to move since being placed in the bed. He sighed softly several times, soothed by the darkness, then allowed his eyes to close and waited for the warm rush of sleep. He felt himself sinking and shifted over to the side where his wife lay sleeping. He moved his arm a little to touch her warm body and found instead the cold metal guard rail of the bed. He opened his eyes a crack, wondering about the harsh cold metal, then shifted to the other side hoping that she had become confused and lay there. The other arm touched cold metal. His wife was missing. His arms ached and the ache grew worse. It moved past the elbows into the shoulders, then down his back into both legs.

The man's eyes opened wide, wider than normal. The room was strange. The bed was strange. There was nothing familiar anywhere. The air was heavy with an alien odor. The pain started moving inward from his aching limbs until it gathered into a great searing hot ball in his middle. He wanted to get up and climb out of the bed with bars on the side. He wanted to walk out of the strange, stuffy room and find his own room with his own bed. He wanted to lie next to his wife where it was safe and familiar, and sleep until all the bad and all the hurt were gone. He grabbed both sides of the bed with his hands and tried to pull himself up. His arms that once lifted hundred-pound packing cases would not respond. He pulled and pulled—waves of agony gushed out of his arms into his chest and stomach—but his body would not rise.

"Help me, help me!" With all the energy inside him, the man shouted out his terror. "Please help me!"

The ceiling light snapped on, blinding the sick man for a moment. "What's the matter? Are you in much pain?" A grey-headed man in a white uniform bent over his bed.

The sick man blinked several times, then whispered, "Doctor, I want to go home."

"I'm not the doctor. But the doctor left orders in case you started having pain. I'll be right back and in a few minutes you'll feel much better."

"Please, please, I want to go home," the sick man gasped as the male nurse turned to go out.

"I'm sorry, sport, but you can't go home tonight. We'll

55

put you to sleep and in the morning you can talk to the doctor. Try and control yourself until I get back. There are others sleeping. OK? I'll be right back."

"I can't go home." He closed his eyes and started whimpering. Pain, exhaustion and loneliness overwhelmed him. It didn't matter if he cried—no one cared—nothing mattered.

The male nurse emptied the syringe into the patient's arm and looked down at the tear-stained face. He studied the sunken eyes and bluish white lips, then turned to go. As he walked back to his desk, he shook his head. "He wants to go home, poor fellow. I better keep a close watch on him—looks like he might be in trouble before the end of the night." The nurse sat down still thinking about his patient. "Be nice if he lasts until his wife has the baby."

# 12

The stillness of her bedroom prevented the woman from falling asleep. She had finally left the hospital after the resident ordered her to go home, reminding her of her responsibility to protect the health of her unborn child by taking care of herself. Riding back on the bus she kept falling asleep, only to be jolted awake repeatedly by the abrupt stops. Once home she fell on her bed; and only by an exercise of will, stimulated by years of habit, was she able to remove her outer clothing, which was left lying in a tangle on the floor.

The softness of the bed and the room's darkness pulled the woman down towards sleep. Her muscles sagged. She sank, but just as she was about to drop below the surface of consciousness something began to tug at her brain. The room was too silent. There were no breathing sounds, no rustlings or belly rumblings. She was in her bedroom all alone; even the baby lay still inside her. Exhausted almost to the point of nausea, the woman could not sleep. The bed felt vast and empty. The absence of another body to counterbalance her weight made her feel as if she might fall off. Finally she shifted until she lay in the middle of the mattress with her head partially on her husband's pillow, partially on her own. She turned her head a little; her nostrils caught the faint odor of his hair and scalp still impregnated in the fabric of the pillow. The odor, instead of bringing a twinge of sadness, made her angry. She was too exhausted to argue with the anger, to tell herself that it was unreasonable. She was angry because her husband was not next to her. That he lay sick in the hospital meant nothing to her at that moment. She needed him and he wasn't there. "I wish to hell he'd hurry up and get well," she muttered. Then hearing the sound of her words and listening to them as if they came from another, she whispered, "What is the matter with me? What kind of a woman am I to be this way when my husband is so sick? It's not his fault." Her voice trailed off and she lay with her eyes open to the darkness. "I'm sorry, honey," she whispered, "it's not your fault."

Fragments of the day's happenings passed through her mind as she lay on her bed unable to sleep. Snatches of conversation, images, bits of feelings. They jumbled together, then sorted out into some kind of logical sequence. The ambulance attendant, the fat woman, the resident, intern and nurse, her husband lying with gadgets stuck all over his body, the white tile and glaring lights, the wailing sound of the ambulance, the groans of her husband, the baby kicking, kicking, kicking inside. All these things had meaning; all these things had happened, but were not real. Nothing was real except the bed, the dark, and the beating of her heart.

The fat lady stood with her hands on her enormous hips. Her breath was like sewer gas, choking and inescapable. "Your husband is sick, mine is too. They made themselves sick. Look at me, how healthy I am; look at you with your baby in your big fat belly. See how healthy you are, and our husbands lie sick. It's their own fault."

"No! No! They don't make themselves sick. It's us; we do it to them, to each other."

The fat lady laughed. "Maybe you're right, maybe you're right. Then make him well."

"I can't. I don't know how!"

"You know how. You keep your baby safe and well inside. Yes, you know how right enough—but you want to save it all for the baby, for the baby, for the baby," she repeated over and over, shrieking with laughter.

"The doctors will make him well, they know how," the young woman screamed back. "Get away from me, you fat old bitch, get away!"

The fat woman lunged forward. "I'll slap your face, you little snip." Her breath blinded and choked with its terrible stench.

"You'll kill the baby, get away." She plunged her hands into her body and pulled out the infant and started beating the fat one across the head and shoulders with it, shrieking, "Get away, get away, you'll kill the baby."

The woman rocked and moaned in her sleep, tugging at the blankets with both hands. Finally her movements ceased as the child inside started kicking, soothing the sleeping woman by its presence.

# 13

Just before sunrise the sick man opened his eyes and tried to remember where he was. Light from the outside was beginning to creep through the curtained window. The room was small, half the size of his own bedroom, but did not feel oppressively small because it lacked furniture. It was empty except for two steel chairs and his bed. He allowed his eyes to search the room, and before he had finished he half remembered being brought in the night before. The sequence of events leading up to his arrival was unclear; it was all vague and, for the time, unimportant. He knew he would remember later on. He lay still, watching the window grow brighter and brighter until at last the rays of the living sun lay on the window, sending him points of brilliance through the fabric of the curtain. The man shifted his head and a sharp twinge of pain reminded him for a moment of the agony his body had endured. His face lay close to a steel washbasin. It was shiny and he could see his features reflected in its surface. The curve of the basin made his face larger than life. His nose was broadened, his thickened lips seemed to join the nose and chin. And his eyes—they were sunken deep in his skull and ringed with dark grey skin.

The man stared at himself for several minutes, then finally

noticed on the other side of the basin a tiny spider struggling to climb up its slippery side. The spider, less than half the size of the nail on the man's little finger, tried over and over to find a foothold on the shiny metal. It would move an inch up the curved surface, then with a desperate thrashing of its threadlike legs slip back. The sick man watched with fascination the tiny creature's exertions. "How did it get here?" he wondered. "In a hospital of all places." He smiled at the spider. "Why did you want to come here?" he asked in a whisper. "You should be out in a garden catching flies or sleeping in the sun. The hospital is only for sick people. You better get out before they find you."

With a slow and very careful movement the man slipped his arm between the bars of the bedguard and reached into the bowl. The movement was painful, but not unbearable. He eased his index finger under the tiny being and pushed it gently to the rim. The spider as it was being lifted curled into a ball, but once on the flat surface it scurried away, disappearing into a crack between the washbowl and the wall.

"It didn't even say thank you," the man giggled, easing his arm back. "I never would have thought of a spider in a hospital." All the events of the day before were now clear, but were not upsetting. The absence of pain and the languid feeling made yesterday's events remote. "Well, you never know. I guess I had a close call. I wonder what I got." He wondered, but for the time he really didn't care. The morning felt good and the deep pain was gone. This was enough for now.

# 14

The resident met the woman just as she was about to enter her husband's room. He led her partway down the hallway by means of hand pressure on her elbow. When they were a sufficient distance from the patient to guarantee privacy, the resident cleared his throat several times.

"Your husband had a good night." He cleared his throat again while the woman bent her head a little to let him know she was listening attentively. "He seems to be relatively free of pain this morning, which is a good sign."

"I haven't seen him yet. I'm glad he's better."

"He's feeling better." The resident picked up the woman's word and used it carefully. "We hope he continues to feel better for a period of time but," he tightened his grip lightly on her elbow, "your husband is a very sick man."

"Yes?" The woman raised her head, looking directly into the doctor's eyes.

"A very sick man." The doctor lifted his eyes just a little, breaking visual contact with the woman. "He has leukemia, acute leukemia."

"Yes?" The woman adjusted her eyes the necessary centimeters to bring them back in contact with the doctor's. Her look said more clearly than any words, 'Tell me everything, tell me the truth. This is no time to be playing games.'

"He has a disease of the blood, of the blood-forming tissue. It's, well, it's a form of cancer."

"Cancer." The woman formed the word soundlessly.

"The white blood cells begin multiplying," the resident started to explain, then stopped himself. "We are doing everything we can."

"What's going to happen to him, doctor?" She hesitated, then in a flattened voice asked, "Is he going to die?"

The resident was about to say in the language of doctors that the patient's condition was grave, but he didn't. Instead, he simply answered, "Yes."

"When?" The woman kept her features and the tone of her voice under tight control.

"There's no way of knowing. All we can do is make an educated guess. If we can bring him to the point of remission—very often by the use of drugs and blood transfusions, patients show a marked improvement—if we can bring your husband to this point, with luck he can be expected to live several months, perhaps as long as a year."

"And if he doesn't have a remission?"

"If he does not have a remission, he cannot be expected to last very long. There's the chance of infection, hemorrhaging; any number of problems can arise." The resident cleared his throat again. "Could be several weeks, possibly sooner. We just don't know about these things. They're always touch and go."

During the course of their conversation the woman had carefully regulated her breathing, which was very shallow. Now she let out all her breath in a sudden, explosive sigh and slowly filled her chest until she could hold no more.

"Do you want to sit down?" The resident moved his hand until it supported the woman's back.

"No, I'll be all right. Don't worry about me. It's just, it's just I can't believe it. How does it happen? Why does it

63

happen?" The woman's voice started to rise. Her chest heaved up and down with increasing rapidity.

"Come, sit down," the resident ordered, guiding the woman to a steel examining stool that was next to the linen closet. "You sit here until you feel better." The resident stood next to her with his hand on her shoulder indicating by its pressure that he was giving her an order.

"Why did it happen, doctor? Why to my—" She was unable to finish the sentence as she struggled against the tears.

"I don't know. Nobody knows. They're working on the problem all over the world. Someday, soon if we're lucky, we'll have the answer, but right now . . ." The doctor shook his head several times instead of completing the sentence. "One of the reasons we brought your husband to this part of the hospital was to keep him under intensive observation so we can learn more about his disease."

"Are you sure he has it?"

"Yes, we're sure. We gave him every test and there can be no doubt. I spoke with your family doctor, and he agrees with the diagnosis."

The numb feeling the woman had experienced the day before after seeing her husband in the emergency room returned. She lost the desire to cry and felt heavy and dull. The baby hung like a lump of iron inside her, pulling on her organs, making her feel bloated and ugly. All of her limbs felt out of proportion and awkward. Somehow, knowledge about her husband's condition was embarrassing. She didn't know what was expected of her or what to say. "What shall I say to him?" she asked in a flat, weary voice. "Does he know?"

"No. He knows nothing. We strongly advise you to tell him nothing." The resident removed his hand from the woman's shoulder. Shifting his position until he stood directly in front of her, he repeated in his most professional voice, "We advise you to tell him nothing! He is very sick, and knowledge that he is suffering from an incurable disease can very possibly upset him and—," the resident softened his tone a bit, "and hasten things. Besides, why should he know? What good would it do?"

There was a long silence while the woman thought about the doctor's words. It took a considerable effort to force all her thoughts together. Finally she responded, but in a voice so soft the doctor had to strain to listen, "I would want to know."

The resident grew very red in the face. "We cannot, of course, forbid you to tell your husband he is dying. That is your right as his wife. But I can tell you that if you let him know, you will be acting contrary to my best medical advice and may be responsible for shortening his life."

"I didn't say I'd tell him." The woman's body started to shake. "It's just that everything is such a shock I don't know what to do; I don't know what to do." She started sobbing softly. "I won't tell him anything, I promise."

The resident gently patted her on the head, handing her a crumpled facial tissue with his other hand. "I'm sorry I upset you. I know these things are hard, very hard. Why don't you go down the hall to the ladies' room and freshen up? You wouldn't want him to see you this way, would you? He's asked about you several times already."

The woman looked up helplessly. Tears were running down her cheeks and mucus dripped unnoticed from her nose. "I don't want to do anything else to hurt him. I promise I won't tell him."

The doctor handed her a second tissue and forced a smile. "He's very weak. Don't spend more than fifteen minutes this time. If all goes well, you can come again in the afternoon."

The woman held the unused tissue in her hand. "Do you think he'll live until the baby is born?" she asked.

The resident hesitated with his answer. He wanted to say

yes, but his training kept the word locked in his throat. "We will do everything in our power to keep him going. If we can get his condition stabilized and there is a remission, we have a good chance he'll last until the baby is born, and possibly for a number of additional months."

As the doctor spoke, the woman started dabbing at her forehead with the tissue. When he finished, she nodded several times but did not look up. She understood.

# 15

The man lying in the hospital bed reminded the woman a little of her husband. She looked at him and smiled and nodded, and he smiled and nodded back. She had been warned by the nurse not to kiss or touch him because of his extreme susceptibility to infection and she was glad for a moment for the nurse's order.

"I can't come too close." She smiled again, speaking louder than usual. "The nurse gave me strict orders not to mix any of my germs with yours."

"That's OK, honey," the man responded weakly. "I wouldn't want you to get too close, might catch what I got. How you doing?"

She nodded in answer to his question. "Do you still have much pain?"

He shook his head. "It's about all gone. They gave me a needle just before, but even without the needle the pain was much better. I've had so many needles in me, I feel like the original human porcupine."

"You look better," the woman lied. "You sure gave me a scare."

"I know," the man grinned back. "Gave myself a pretty good scare too. Thank God I'm getting better."

"Did you sleep good?" the woman asked, wondering what she should say next and beginning to feel uncomfortable.

"Yeah, I slept OK," the man mumbled awkwardly. "How about you?"

"I'll sleep a lot better when you come home." The words flowed easily. The woman experienced a moment of satisfaction at their casual sound. "I miss your little noises and your tossing and turning."

"I know. I missed you too. I'll sure be glad to get the hell out of this place—it gives me the creeps."

The conversation stopped and they looked at each other. Both continued to smile, but neither one knew what else to say.

As she looked, the woman started to examine the man's face. She knew he was her husband, but he felt like someone she had known long ago. Her feelings at the moment were feelings similar to those she had toward her dead grandfather. He was a person she had known long ago, someone to whom she once felt close, someone she missed on those rare occasions when his memory rose up from its resting place. As she scrutinized her husband's features, the woman wondered at the strangeness of her reaction. She remembered the dead man's face as he lay in the funeral parlor. It didn't look like her grandfather. It looked like someone pretending to be her grandfather—waxen and very old. Her sick husband's sunken eyes and grey waxen skin only reminded her of the man she married. Even the hair was different, lifeless and dull. Her knowledge that he would soon be gone added to the growing feeling of strangeness.

The man waited for his wife to speak. He was weary. The brief conversation had taxed his limited reserve of energy leaving him only strength enough to hold his eyes open. He watched the woman's face, trying to read what she was feeling from her expression. "She's very upset," he told himself, taking care to keep his own features immobile. "She is putting on a brave front, but she is upset, I can tell." He was pleased with his wife's apparent ability to control her emotions. This fit his notions about bravery. When a person was sick or in serious trouble, that was the time other members of the family had to exercise self-control.

As the sick man thought about his wife's display of self-control, without his being aware of what was happening part of his mind drifted away. It was as if his thoughts had split in half. One half concentrated on the woman standing near his bed, the other half going toward the other woman with whom he had once been intimate. His mother would never let herself appear upset when he got sick. Once when his toe became infected and the nail had to be removed, she assisted the doctor who came to the house and did not turn her head as he cut into the tissue. As the man examined his wife's composed features and thought about his mother, for a moment, for the briefest part of a moment, he felt a cold hollowness inside.

"I'm not supposed to stay too long, the doctor said." The awkwardness of the long silence forced her to speak. "Anything I can do for you before I go?"

The man grinned. He was going to say nothing, but instead hesitated, grinning until he blushed, then whispered, "Let me feel the baby."

The woman stiffened. She felt as if some strange unhealthy old man wanted to molest her. After several seconds of hesitation, bringing herself under control, she moved close to the bed. The sick man forced his hand between the bars of the bedguard, placing the palm against his wife's abdomen. Neither one moved for the space of a minute.

The woman shifted her eyes from her husband's face to his hand. Unlike his face, it had not changed. She looked at his hand and murmured to herself, her lips barely moving,

69

"This man is your husband." She moved a half step closer so that her body was pressed tight against the hand.

"Jesus Christ," the man gurgled, his cheekbones showing a faint flush of pink, "I can feel the little bastard. I can feel him. What a strange thing."

His exertion was too much. His hand dropped down and was left hanging out of the bed. The woman carefully picked up the hand and maneuvered it between the bars, placing it on her husband's chest. Then without saying another word she turned and went out of the room.

"I could feel it move." The thought spilled from the man's mind and poured through his body. He closed his eyes tight, allowing himelf to feel the thought. "He was pounding with his little fists and kicking with his feet. 'Let me out. Let me out.'" The man chuckled. "'I want to get out and see my daddy.'" The man nodded his head, still keeping his eyes tightly shut. "Just be patient, little fellow. It won't be long now, only a couple of months." Like warm milk, the thoughts filled his body. His fingers and toes started to tingle. The tingling sensation began traveling up his arms and legs. "Just be patient, little baby; you have to grow fat and strong before you can come out." The tingling was mixed with tiny needle points of pain. "'Let me out. Let me out. I want to get out and see my daddy before he dies.'" The man gasped as the insane mouse started its frantic dance inside his stomach.

# 16

The woman hesitated on the street just outside the hospital gates. She had the balance of the morning and part of the afternoon before her next visit. She thought of returning home, of taking a walk or going shopping, but decided not to decide just then. She had all the time in the world. The sun warmed the frosty air and made her face glow. Despite the city noise, everything seemed still. The little room where her husband lay might have been a thousand miles away.

She looked at the great sprawling hospital. It was an ugly place, but a place where she did not have to live. The sight of the hospital repelled her, and she started walking down the hill. She closed her eyes against the sun's rays and felt their hot orange and reds through her lids. "I wonder if he will last until the baby comes." The resident's careful response to her question floated into her mind. "He didn't say yes or no. He said there's a chance he'll last till the baby comes." She tried to remember the doctor's exact words. "He said if he has a remission, there is a good chance. I wonder if those doctors really know what they're doing?" The thought was not upsetting. It was just another in a series of interrelated thoughts. "Maybe they're just a bunch of grown-ups playing at being doctors." The woman blushed and deepened her breathing a little as her thinking shifted to a game of doctor played in her backyard years ago. Before the scene could sharpen she forced it away and turned her thoughts back to her conversation with the resident. "I suppose they know what they are doing— all that schooling. Wonder why anyone would want to spend his life dealing with sickness? The smell of those places makes me sick." The resident's features grew sharp in the woman's mind. She saw him standing over her with his hand on her shoulder. "Maybe they like sickness. Maybe it's not only that they want to make people well, maybe some of them really like all that mess. Maybe they don't even know it themselves." The sun's rays burnt into her eyes, finally forcing her to look down at the sidewalk. "I wonder if it is a fifty-fifty chance," the woman mused, going over the resident's words again. She stopped walking and examined a tiny crack in the sidewalk. All the other squares were perfect except this one. The crack was irregular and there was no apparent reason for its existence. It was just there.

Suddenly, the woman felt her skin prickle as a painful cold sensation spread from her chest through her entire body. She shuddered and pulled her coat tighter around her shoulders. The sun seemed to have lost much of its warmth and the frosty air tugged at her face and hands. Then with a force that left her trembling, the realization struck that her husband was going to die. Until that moment it had all been words. The man in the hospital bed had not been real. Her sobs when the resident told her were for the idea, not for the reality. "Your husband is going to die; in a little while you will be a widow." Her insides sank and she wanted to run away and hide and cry and tell herself it was not really true. "He may not even live to see the baby." Her whispered words turned into sobs. "He may be dying right now. Oh my God!" The woman turned around and started running back up the hill unmindful of the tears that were freezing on her cheeks and of the thrashing baby in her body.

She pushed through the double doors, the only entrance with which she was familiar, and looked wildly in every direction. She spotted the angular-faced nurse who had worked on her husband and ran up to her and grabbed her sleeve. "I want to see the doctor. Please," she begged, forcing the words through her sobs, "let me speak to the doctor, for a minute. I must speak to him."

After one look at the woman's face, the nurse quickly nodded and led her into the examining room. The tired-eyed intern recognized the hysterical woman and took both of her hands in his. "What's the matter, what's the matter?" Still holding her hands, he led her to the examining table and forced her to sit on its edge.

"He's going to die." Her words came out in gulps as the woman's body shuddered. "The other doctor told me my husband has leukemia." Each word was punctuated by a convulsive sob.

The intern tightened his jaw, preventing his face from showing any emotion. He was able to control his facial expression but was unable to stop his hands from sweating. "We are doing everything in our power," he said awkwardly, ashamed of his words, knowing that they did not answer the woman's needs. "He's getting the best possible care."

"Do you think he'll live until the baby is born, doctor?" She looked at the puffy eyes and clenched jaw of the young man standing in front of her. "It's not too long," she begged.

Instead of answering, the intern tightened his grip on the woman's hands. After a minute of silence broken only by the woman's sobs, he murmured, "Everyone in the hospital who knows about it wants your husband to live until the child is born. Although to you and him it is everything, to us, to me," the intern paused, groping for the right words, "to me, it is very important also. I want your husband to live to see his child, believe me when I say it."

As the doctor was speaking, the nurse turned her face partially away. She chewed on her lower lip, then on her upper, and kept rubbing the palms of her hands against the sides of her uniform.

With a deep sigh that caused her body to quiver, the woman freed her hands and forced herself to her feet. "I'm sorry I acted so silly." As she spoke her head sank until her chin rested on her chest. "It all just hit me at once—I didn't know what to do."

"You don't have to say another word. I understand." The intern smiled, then signaled the nurse to lead the trembling woman out into the corridor.

During the minute that the nurse was gone the intern remained standing, lacing and unlacing the fingers of his hands. When the nurse reentered the room, she took one look at the young man and hesitated. His face was a deep scarlet and his features appeared to be twisted with rage.

"I had one of the orderlies take her to the main waiting room." The nurse stopped speaking and without being aware of what she was doing backed up several inches. "What's the matter doctor? You look like you're about to explode. Are you getting sick?"

"No!" The intern raised his voice until he was almost shouting. "I am not getting sick. I am sick! Sick and disgusted with this whole lousy business. Sick of all the damn misery in this world."

"It's no one's fault that her husband is going to die," the nurse responded lamely.

"No one's fault her husband is going to die," the young doctor mimicked the nurse, irrationally turning a portion of his anger toward her. "We're a bunch of hypocrites, that's what we are. We like to play God. We've got them all believing that we can dispense life and health. Shit! We can't even cure a common cold."

"There's no need to shout, doctor." The nurse felt herself growing angry. She understood the man's distress, but didn't like being mimicked. "There are patients waiting and you'll be heard out in the hall."

"I don't give a damn!" The months of short sleep and the constant pressure had eroded the young doctor's judgment. "We're a bunch of coldblooded bastards. Worrying about getting an autopsy release and at the same time telling her that we will do everything in our power to keep him going until the baby is born."

"Autopsy release?" The nurse raised her eyebrows.

"My worthy senior colleague is worried she might not allow a p.m. on this 'interesting case.' He says he is going to tell her how important it is for medical science and all the rest."

"Well? What's wrong with that?" The nurse put her hands on her hips and raised her shoulders a little. "I don't see anything wrong with being realistic. Making plans so his wife will cooperate at the proper time doesn't affect him."

"Yes it does!" The intern tightened his hands into fists.

"You're being ridiculous, doctor." The older woman dismissed the young man's petulant words with a toss of her head. She had better things to do than argue with a kid scarcely out of medical school.

"Our damn coldbloodedness breeds death. We talk about keeping a patient alive but at the same time think about what we are going to find when we do an autopsy. I'm sick of all this pain and death and disease. Why does there have to be so much suffering? Why does a kid like that have to die? It's all a big rotten mess and I'm right here in the middle of it."

The nurse turned away and went out into the hall. "If he

can't stand the heat, let him get out of the kitchen," she muttered under her breath. "As if he were the only one who wants to see the kid last until the baby comes. All that stuff about pain and disease. Nobody forced him to be a doctor." She hesitated outside the door adjusting her uniform with tiny finger tugs. "We all do everything we can." She felt her cap to make sure it was on straight. "And there's plenty who deserve everything they get. Plenty who ask for it—still we do everything we can." Without realizing it, the nurse raised her voice to a normal speaking level and snapped, "And most aren't the least bit grateful." An orderly who was passing turned his head at the nurse's words, then quickly turned away when he saw her face.

# 17

As the woman entered the main waiting room she saw her fat acquaintance of the day before sitting at the far end. Each simultaneously avoided the other's eyes; the young woman deliberately chose a chair facing in the opposite direction. She sank into the chair and closed her eyes trying to push the heaviness out of her mind. The warmth of the waiting room, together with her emotional exhaustion, made it easy for her to slip into a light doze. Threads of the dream of the night before became entangled with her present dozing state. The resident telling her the diagnosis, her husband lying in a crib-like bed too feeble to move his dangling hand, the fat woman's grating voice.

"Did you figure out how to keep him alive?"

The woman forced her eyes open and tried to focus them on the swollen form in front of her. She rubbed the back of her hand across her face. "What did you say?" It was as if the fat woman had materialized out of the dream.

"Did you figure out how to keep him alive?" she repeated, leaning close to the half-awake woman, spraying drops of saliva into her face.

The seated woman sat bolt upright, her eyes widening in fright. "What do you mean?" she whispered.

"Yesterday you said it was your thoughts that made him sick. If you made him sick, then make him well."

"You said," the young woman started shaking so that her teeth chattered, "do I know how to keep him alive?"

"No I didn't, dearie, you must have been dreaming. I asked if you know how to make him well—I said nothing about keeping him alive. How could I know that he is dying?"

"Why are you doing this to me?" The young woman pushed down into the chair, afraid to get up.

"Doing what to you?" The fat woman stepped back a pace and held her hands out with the palms turned up. "I'm only trying to be friendly. No point in two people who are in the same boat quarreling. Is he really dying?"

The seated woman nodded her head. Her throat had grown so tight she couldn't speak.

"Do you think he'll last until the baby is born?" Without waiting for an answer, the fat lady continued, "Well, at least he has that. When mine goes, there'll be nothing left of him. Yours will have a piece of himself still alive, at least he'll have that."

The fear that had overwhelmed the younger woman started to diminish. "She's crazy, poor thing," she told herself. "I mustn't let her upset me."

"You see what you can do to keep him alive." The fat woman admonished. "But keep your eyes on all the others— remember what you said to me yesterday. It's everybody's bad thoughts, even strangers. You try hard, honey, but you may need help, especially in this damn place." The fat woman took another step backward and started to turn away, then turned back for a moment. "I still think your theory is a lot of crap—they do it to themselves. But you keep trying. I'll stay in touch and we'll see who is right."

The woman clasped her hands and rested them on her swollen abdomen. As she stared at them, she realized that she had adhered to her resolve of the day before, not to feel the baby until her husband got well. She felt a tiny glow of satisfaction at her self-discipline, then almost immediately experienced a sinking sensation as she realized the futility of it all.

She tightened the grip of her hands, trying to control their tremor. "She scared me out of my wits." The woman turned her head to see if the fat woman was hovering nearby. "Am I glad she's gone," she whispered to herself. "She's out of her mind. Maybe her husband's sickness was too much for her." In some subtle fashion the woman derived a measure of satisfaction from her own words. "The poor thing is cracking up under the strain." She nodded, agreeing with herself. "Well, I can't allow myself to go to pieces, there's more than me to consider. There is the baby. A piece of him inside of me." The woman's mouth opened in wonder. "A piece of him really is inside me!" Until that moment, in spite of the words she might have spoken, she felt that the growing baby was hers alone. The night of conception had never seemed important. Hunching down in the chair, the woman buried her face in her hands and whispered over and over, "Please, God, let him live to see his baby. Please, God."

# 18

The resident frowned and pressed his lips together until they began to turn bluish white. As he felt for the sick man's pulse, he raised his eyes and visually checked the rate of flow in the blood transfusion equipment. He shifted his eyes to the patient. "Do you feel any better? How's your stomach?"

The sick man nodded, moving his head scarcely more than an inch. "I feel woozy," he whispered. "Feels like everything is wavy—like the ocean."

"How's your stomach?" The resident placed his free hand on the sick man's abdomen and started probing cautiously. "Any place hurt worse than the other?"

"It doesn't hurt—it feels funny, but it doesn't hurt." The sick man closed his eyes for several seconds, trying to concentrate on his insides. "Before you gave me that needle, it felt like I was about to tear to pieces." The man forced a wan smile. "The only way I can say it is it's like a mouse running round and round and digging its toenails into me harder and harder."

The resident stopped probing and checked the patient's pulse against his wristwatch. "You'll be all right. This one wasn't too bad. You lost a little blood, but it looks like everything's under control." Still frowning, he stood up and surveyed the patient. "You must not let yourself get upset or excited. I understand you had your, ah," he increased the severity of his frown, "your little setback just after your wife left. We want to allow her to see you, but it's up to you to avoid speaking about or thinking about things that are upsetting. We will limit her visits to ten minutes at a time for the next few days."

The sick man felt vaguely guilty as he listened to the other's words. He wondered if the resident knew he had felt the baby and, if he knew, would his wife get into trouble?

"It's very important for you to remain as quiet as possible so that your body has a chance to start repairing itself. Rest and sleep are your best medicine." The resident walked over to the window and made a slight adjustment to the curtain, eliminating a sliver of light. He took one final look at the patient, snapped off the light and left the room.

He hesitated in the corridor, listening intently for any unnatural sounds, then started to walk away. After he had taken several steps, he stopped and eased back to the partially open door.

He listened outside the door for almost a minute, then shook his head as he thought about the patient. "This kid is in real trouble. I don't like the way he looks. If he picks up an infection . . . Might be better if I keep his wife away and reduce the risk. Keep her away for a few days and see how he does." The resident started walking down the corridor toward the nurse's station. Halfway there he stopped, still deep in thought. "If I don't let his wife come, he'll get upset and start fussing. She might insist; it would be hard to keep her away if she insists. No point in antagonizing her for nothing. I'll have her wear a sterile gown and face mask—better have everyone keep sterile. If I can keep him from getting infected, I think I can keep him going for a while." The resident started sucking at a bit of meat that had lodged between his teeth.

81

He nodded his head. "If I can keep him going for a week, he's good for a couple of months at least. Christ! Half the hospital staff already knows about this case. That baby is going to end up being the hospital mascot."

The resident thought about the patient's wife. He visualized her distended abdomen and her pale tear-stained face. "I don't know why everyone is making such a fuss about whether he lives to see the baby or not." The resident shrugged. "What the hell difference does it really make? Even if he does live, he'll be gone before the kid is old enough to crawl. All that crap about a part of you living on after you're gone. As if it made any difference. When you're dead, you're dead, and if you have twenty children and a hundred and twenty grandchildren, it doesn't make you one little bit less dead. The trick is in staying alive. When you're dead, you're a piece of human garbage. One second after you're gone, it's as if you never were." His thoughts caused the resident to breathe deeply and he felt a stab of pain over his left nipple. "I'm going to keep that kid going because that's my job." The resident's thoughts turned into whispered words. "I'm a doctor and it's my responsibility to do everything to preserve his life. Whether he lives to see the baby—that's irrelevant. Nothing but a bunch of romantic nonsense."

The resident felt a hand on his shoulder and turned around. His first reaction was one of irritation as he saw the smiling face of the patient's family doctor.

"How is he?" the older doctor asked in a sonorous voice. "I would have been in earlier, but my office was full. Besides," he patted the younger man's arm, "I knew he was in good hands."

The resident forced himself to reply civilly to the other's question. He resented having to share his patient. "He had another hemorrhage, not as bad as the first, but I'm worried. If he picks up an infection, we're in trouble."

The older doctor shook his head and made a clucking noise. "What a shame. How's his wife taking it?"

"I told her the facts this morning. She's all right. What you might expect—some crying, but she handled it pretty well. I told her not to tell him anything."

"You don't think he should know?" The older man raised his eyebrows.

"I want to keep him alive. If he finds out what's wrong, he may not be able to handle it. No point in taking chances. Besides, what difference does it make?" The resident spoke in a matter-of-fact manner, taking particular care to hide his irritation.

"I don't know. I don't know. I suppose you're right. Probably would have come to the same decision myself." The older man started tapping his forefinger on his lips. "I generally tell them the truth if they really want to know. If they don't ask, I say nothing. But if they press me—though in this case with things so touch and go I can see your point. No unnecessary chances. We want to do everything to keep him alive until the baby is born."

"Yes, we want to keep him alive until the baby is born," the resident echoed woodenly.

"I'll look in on the patient just to say hello. I'm sure you've done everything that needs doing."

"He may be sleeping," the resident warned.

"If he is sleeping, young man," the older doctor dropped his smile and allowed a threatening edge to enter his voice, "I will not awaken him. I appreciate your concern for my patient, but I can assure you that even without your warning I would have tried to exercise sound judgment."

The older doctor eased into the sick man's room and waited motionless while his eyes grew used to the semi-darkness. He listened carefully to the patient's breathing, trying to judge from the sound whether the man was awake or asleep.

Taking a step closer he peered at the reclining figure.

"Hi," the sick man whispered. "It's all right, I'm not sleeping."

The doctor leaned over the bed and inspected the transfusion needle. He pulled out his stethoscope and after listening to the man's heart, sat down on the edge of the bed. "I heard you weren't feeling too well this morning." For the first time the doctor spoke to the man in a normal conversational tone. "I'm sorry I didn't get here sooner. I had a large number of patients to see and I knew you were in the best of hands."

"That's OK, doc, they're taking good care of me. I'm getting as much attention as a movie star."

"I don't want to tire you." The doctor started to get up.

"Don't go yet." The man forced his voice above a whisper. "Please don't go yet." There was a pleading sound to his voice.

The doctor sank back heavily on the bed and placed his hand on the patient's. "I'll stay another minute, but I have to go soon. I have several other patients to see and we don't want to tire you, do we?" The bedside manner began to insinuate itself into the doctor's voice.

"What's wrong with me? Nobody says. They've given me all those tests and nobody tells me anything."

"We're not sure." The doctor patted the man's hand. "An acute viral infection of some sort. One of those rare bugs that spring up from time to time. With complete bed rest and some blood to replace what you've lost, you should be up and about before long." The doctor looked at the wall as he spoke, glad for the darkness in the room.

"That crazy feeling inside my stomach, like a mouse; that scares me, doc."

"Some minor liver and spleen involvement. Those viruses often do that. It feels a lot worse than it is. I better be going

84

now. The important thing is to rest and regain your strength —don't start worrying and upset yourself for nothing."

As the doctor walked to the door, the man called after him, "Thanks, doc, you've taken a load off my mind. I was beginning to think it was something fatal."

After the doctor had gone, the man let out several deep sighs, then resumed his regular breathing pattern. The doctor's words filled the sick man's mind and he savored them with the same delight he had known ten years earlier when by chance he overheard two teachers talking about him. He had remained behind in the class after the other students were dismissed, to put away some demonstration equipment. Within a few minutes the school building grew silent and occasional footfalls or voices out in the hallway were magnified. He was getting ready to go when he heard his name mentioned by a teacher with whom he'd had a class the year before. This teacher was talking to one of his present instructors. Words such as, "thoughtful, considerable latent ability, shows promise," had filled his ears like golden bubbles sending waves of satisfaction rippling through his body. For years his teacher's words were an inexhaustible supply of stimulating fuel whenever he was burdened with doubt about himself. Unlike words of encouragement or praise from his parents or close friends, his teacher's praise was completely believable.

The doctor's brief conversation with him left the sick man feeling content and safe. He had listened carefully, trying to detect any false note in the doctor's voice. It all sounded logical and real. "A severe virus." The man nodded to himself. "That's why it felt like the flu, a severe flu. 'Some liver and spleen involvement'; that's why my insides acted so funny. He didn't try to make believe it was nothing. He admitted they didn't know what virus—you don't die from a virus— unless you catch pneumonia—and then they have all those new wonder drugs." The man began to grin. He had carefully analyzed the doctor's statement and each word stood the test of scrutiny. He now had the necessary knowledge to cope with the pain, the weakness and the strange abdominal disturbance.

"Christ, that made me feel a lot better." The man adjusted his position in bed, disregarding the pains in his limbs. "As long as I know I'll make it, I can stand the rest." For a moment he was proud of himself. He would show them how he could handle pain. It was going to be easy to be brave now that he knew everything would be all right.

Disregarding the ache and the deep bone cold of his arms and legs, the man closed his eyes and let himself sink. It was intoxicating to be rid of the fear that had gnawed at him for the past day and a half. Even the peculiar sensation in his abdomen was not sufficient to keep him awake. "Run, you little son of a bitch," he mumbled just before falling asleep. "You don't bother me any more."

# 19

It was early evening when the woman finally was able to see her husband. He had slept deeply and looked better and more at ease than earlier in the day. As a precaution against infection the woman was dressed in a sterile white smock and had a gauze mask covering her mouth and nose. When she first entered the room, her husband did not recognize her and scarcely acknowledged her presence. She took a chair on the other side of the room and waited, thinking he might be too tired to speak. Then from the man's vacant expression she realized he did not know who she was. "You're a fine one," she bantered, "not recognizing your own wife."

Startled, the man raised his head several inches. "Well, I'll be," he chuckled, letting his head fall back on the pillow. "You look like a pregnant Florence Nightingale."

"Now is that nice?" She adjusted the smock so that it did not billow out quite so far in front.

"When you came in," he teased in a weak but happy voice, "I wondered where they got that big fat nurse. Most of the ones I've seen are on the skinny side and look like their faces have been dried in the sun like prunes."

" 'Big fat nurse,' you've got your nerve." The tension the woman had been under as she entered the room evaporated. She laughed and her laughter was not forced.

"You do look pretty cute in that outfit." The man lifted his head again, surveying his wife. "Maybe you missed your calling. Instead of getting married you should have dedicated yourself to the care of suffering humanity."

The woman quipped back, "Taking care of you has been a dedication to suffering humanity." As soon as the words were out of her mouth, she froze, afraid she had said the wrong thing.

The man chuckled, and his wife's fear instantly dissolved. "I guess I have been a handful. Well, I don't believe in fooling around. If you are going to get sick, might as well do it right." The short conversation used up the man's limited store of energy and left him exhausted and breathing rapidly.

"One of these days you'll have your turn and then we'll see what kind of a nurse you are." The woman forced a laugh, wondering if her husband could tell it was forced.

"I had a talk with the doctor before." The man spoke softly.

"Which one?"

"The one who came to the house. I asked him what was wrong with me."

The woman tensed, then in a carefully controlled voice asked, "What did he say?"

"He didn't talk to you?" The man sounded surprised.

"No. Not yet. I plan to call him later on."

"He said I had a very bad virus and that my liver and spleen are involved. He said that if I avoid getting an infection, I'll be all right."

"I'm so glad, honey." The woman regulated her voice carefully, but it was a little too loud. "I knew you would be all right. Once I got you to the hospital, I knew they would know what to do."

The man grinned and started to speak, but was interrupted by a weak spell of coughing. After the coughing subsided he grinned again as he whispered, "For a time there I thought I was going to die. This morning after you left, I would have sworn that I had something fatal. It just shows you how much worrying you do for nothing."

"The resident told me that the worst thing for you to do is worry and get yourself upset. I hope you have learned your lesson." The woman got up and was about to go over to the bed when she stopped herself. "They gave me strict instructions not to get too close," she said apologetically. "I'll make it up to you when you get better—I promise."

Although tired by his wife's visit, the man did not want to fall asleep after she had gone. Something about their conversation left him uneasy, but he did not know what. He looked up at the transfusion bottle. The dark red liquid dripped from the bottle into a little glass chamber, then traveled down a length of transparent plastic tubing until it finally entered his body. The bottle was almost empty and the man was certain that it would be replaced by a full one before long. "It seems like they're putting a lot more blood into me than I lost," he mused, trying to estimate the number of bottles he had received. He shrugged and didn't pursue the thought. Much of the time he had been asleep or unconscious, and it was an effort to try to calculate the time it took a bottle to empty. He watched the drops fall and noticed that they were almost in perfect synchronization with his heartbeats. "I wonder if they do that on purpose," he thought. "They seem to know what they're doing."

The man still felt uneasy and turned his eyes away from the dripping blood, which was beginning to produce a hypnotic effect. "You'd think she would ask them what was wrong with me. She acted like she didn't know anything." His thoughts kept tugging at his brain. "She said she was going to call the doctor tonight—he was very busy, he told me that he had to see several patients. But what about the resident?" the man asked himself. "He could have told her. Maybe she didn't see him."

He was about to give up the struggle to remain awake when he felt the skin tighten on the back of his neck. The physical message came an instant before he remembered: his wife said the resident told her that the worst thing would be if he got upset. "They did talk," he whispered. "He must have spoken to her about what is wrong with me. She must have asked him. I can't believe she didn't ask him." The tightening sensation began to spread and he became aware of a tingling in his toes and fingers. These signs served as a warning and the sick man told himself, "Calm down, calm down, don't get yourself upset." In spite of his warning, the thoughts kept tugging at his brain until they felt like tweezers inside his skull. "If she knew about me, why did she act as if she didn't know? She must be hiding something. There must be something she doesn't want me to know." He forced himself halfway up in the bed and spoke out loud, "No, don't let yourself panic, think it through. Remember what the doctor said about it being a virus. But she saw the resident—Oh!" The man let out his breath explosively, his head falling back onto the pillow. "She didn't say when she spoke to him. She didn't say she spoke to him today. Might have been yesterday— some time yesterday before they finished making all those tests. Might have been any time before he was sure."

The man closed his eyes, trying to force the tingling sensation to recede. His heart was beating very rapidly and inside his abdomen there was a stirring. He opened his eyes, focusing them on the dripping blood. His heartbeats and the blood were no longer synchronized.

As the sick man struggled to control himself, the night nurse entered the room. He took one look at the patient and reached for the oxygen mask. "Short of breath?" he asked, opening the control valve.

90

"No," whispered the sick man, shaking his head at the same time. "It was just a little pain, it's going away now. I'll be all right."

The male nurse shut the valve and replaced the breathing mask. "You looked like you were having some difficulty when I came in."

"My stomach, it felt funny for a minute."

"How you doing?" The nurse made some small adjustments to the bedcovers. "You weren't feeling too red-hot last night."

"I wanted to go bowling this evening," the man chuckled softly, "but the doctor felt I might ruin my average. He advised me to wait another couple of days."

"Yeah, I guess you would have trouble bowling more than three or four lines in your condition." The nurse joined in the banter without changing his facial expression or tone of voice.

"I'd have a hell of a time picking up a really tough split this evening. Though you never know, a quality player shouldn't let a mild illness throw him off his game."

"Better wait another day or two." The nurse pretended to be offering a profound medical opinion, mimicking the behavior of certain doctors he had known. "The human body has remarkable recuperative powers and medical science has progressed enormously in the past decade—but after two hemorrhages, I think it wise to wait a day or two before resuming your regular bowling schedule."

"I want to make a confession." The sick man, completely exhausted, was only able to whisper. "If I were in the bowling alley right now, instead of me rolling the ball down the lane, it would roll me. A slow game of marbles . . ."

The other man held his finger up to his lips. "No more talking," he said, crinkling his eyes into a smile. "You sound like your battery is run down. A good night's sleep and you'll be ready for that bowling game."

91

"Marbles." The sick man formed the word with his lips.

"OK, marbles. That's what we need here in the hospital. A marbles championship." The nurse chuckled. "Half the people here could qualify, staff included. Half the people here have lost their marbles. We could have a hell of a championship."

The sick man grinned and nodded. He felt close to the other man and believed they were becoming friends. He motioned the nurse to come closer, then whispered, "What's wrong with me?" counting on the developing friendship to produce an honest response.

"You're sick," the nurse whispered back. "Now I don't want to hear another word out of you. If you want to get well soon, you need lots of sleep."

The man closed his eyes and lay still, waiting until the nurse had left. When he heard the click of the light switch, he lifted his free hand to his mouth and bit the knuckle of his forefinger to muffle the sobs that tore out of his chest. He lay alone in the dark and cried until exhaustion finally forced him into sleep.

Out in the hallway the nurse stood listening to the muted sounds of crying. He looked at his watch several times and once made as if to reenter the room. When at last the room was still, he tiptoed carefully down the corridor to his station, his eyes narrowed to tiny slits. "Bowling," he muttered. "The poor kid will never lift another bowling ball in this world." He sat down at his table, opened a drawer and fished out the man's medical record. "We're playing the hospital-doctor-nurse game of 'let's not tell' with that poor bastard." His eyes remained narrowed in anger. "But we don't score like they do in any other game. We know who is going to win or lose in advance." The nurse opened the folder and scanned its contents. "We don't even ask the principal player if he wants to play."

The nurse pushed his chair back and stared at the frost-etched window. He thought about the thousands of patients who had moved through the hospital during the years of his employment and of the hundreds he had known. "Some of the incurable ones don't want to know," he mused. "You can tell. They don't ask questions. Even when they are close to the end and have to be fed through tubes, they don't ask. If the patient wants to play, that's fine. Or if a patient starts to probe and gets a sniff of the truth and then decides that he would rather not know for sure, that's OK too." The nurse studied the complex pattern of frost on the pane for a moment and for a moment wondered about its complexity. "If they want to know, if they keep asking the right questions so you know they really want to know—that's where the game should stop."

The nurse picked up the folder again and read the resident's handwritten instructions and evaluation of the case. "How does he know?" the nurse muttered. "Maybe if that kid knew the truth, he'd feel better than wondering. Maybe it would make him worse, but it's his right to know. It's his life, and you can't really fool them. Those who want to know, sooner or later they find out enough—sure, they can't be certain; there's always a little doubt, but they know. It's a rotten game, and this time we have an added attraction. This game is the biggest of them all. This one is being played with the great golden basketball. Keep the patient alive until the baby is born, but don't tell him anything. I wonder if we should sell chances, how close will he come. Might raise enough money to send the kid to college." The nurse put away the folder and stood up. "That poor guy. Thank God it isn't me."

93

# 20

The man listened to the early morning sounds of the hospital. He had been awake for many minutes, but did not want to come out of the darkness. He felt as if he had aged twenty years during the night. His insides seemed swollen and old.

The man turned his head a little as he heard someone enter the room. For a moment his eyes refused to focus and he waited for the visitor to speak. "How are you doing, man?" It was the Negro orderly who had brought him to the room. "How are you doing?" the orderly repeated.

"Rotten," the man croaked, surprised at his own voice. "Feel like I'm not long for this world."

"Who is long for this world?" the black man shrugged. "Ain't none of us gonna last another hundred years. You," he jutted his chin, wrinkling his forehead at the same time, "probably got another thirty, forty, fifty years. Maybe sixty if you're lucky, but I doubt it."

"Don't try and kid me." The man's voice still was thick and guttural, "Way I feel, I'll be lucky to last a year."

"Stop eating at yourself, man. Most patients sick enough to be in the hospital feel like that at first. Some of the older ones don't make it. But at your age—shit. You feel bad, but in a few days you'll feel different."

"Do you really think so?" the man pleaded rather than asked.

"I've been around this place long enough to tell the difference between those who are gonna make it or not. With heart attacks you can't be too sure for several days, but with the rest —if you were all that bad, we wouldn't be talking right now."

"I guess you're right. It feels worse than it is. I just never expected to be in any hospital. I never thought about getting sick."

The orderly nodded his head vigorously. "I work in a hospital. I've worked in a hospital for five years but I'll tell you one thing, I don't want to be *in* no hospital. I know just what you mean. And if I was you, I would put all of my mind on getting well so that I could get out of this place and go back to my own private abode. And another thing, remember the words to that old song? 'Accentuate the positive, eliminate the negative.' That's a good thing to keep in mind. I've seen a lot of patients stay here twice as long as they should because they kept themselves sick by worrying."

The man listened carefully to the orderly's words. They soothed him and filled many of the empty doubting places in his mind. This man wasn't bluffing or trying to hide the truth. This man would know if he were critically ill, and the way he talked it was easy to tell that he wasn't worried. The sick man croaked out as the orderly left the room, "Come by again if you get a chance, any time at all."

The orderly stopped by the nurse's station for a moment after he left. The male nurse was making some final entries into patients' charts before his relief arrived. "Just looked in on the patient in Room 208." The orderly lowered his voice as he spoke.

"Is he still sleeping?"

"No, he's awake. We talked for a minute. He don't look too good. Think he'll make it till the baby is born?"

"How should I know?" The nurse yawned and started rubbing his eyes. "If he does, it won't be by much."

"I'll come back by this evening before I start my shift. I think I cheered him up a little."

"That's OK with me. If you can make him feel any better, that's all right with me."

"Glad I'm not in his shoes." The orderly spoke half to himself. "You see a fellow like that and it makes you wonder. Sure am glad I ain't in his shoes."

# 21

From a thousand places throughout the city people rose up from their beds and prepared themselves for their day's work among the sick and dying. This was a varied group, those who labored at the thousand chores in the great sprawling hospital. Fresh-faced young girls who did the typing—vast quantities of records and correspondence telling of disease, of pain, of recovery, of death. To these women the hospital was a flood of paper and a place where eligible bachelors existed in extraordinary profusion. There were those who dealt with tissue and serum—lab assistants, technicians, microbiologists; to them the hospital was blood and biopsies, urine and feces. There were the janitors and the matrons, all poor and mostly black. The hospital for them was endless soiled bathrooms, scuffed floors and dingy windows. There were many others scrubbing sleep out of their eyes, eating breakfast, reading the morning newspaper before their day's work began. Young doctors looking forward to moderate wealth and considerable status, pleased with themselves and with the knowledge painfully squeezed into their heads. Nurses largely dissatisfied, underpaid and with little status, on whose backs the hospital really rested. And then there were the few who worked in the morgue, those who dealt exclusively with death. They arrived each day confident that their fair share of work would be waiting.

Who were these people who spent each day in this house of sickness, whose livelihood derived from pain and pestilence? Were they different from the others in the city to whom the very thought of the hospital was enough to cause distress? Every person who worked in the hospital, from the janitor scrubbing a urinal to the hospital chief in his grand leather chair, might say that his work was in the service of the sick and suffering. But so might the rat catchers wandering in the sewers, the guards ringing the prisons, the diggers of graves and the judges of criminals. So might the policemen with execution on their hips, the preachers with damnation in their mouths. Each might say that he in his own way served humanity. Who could refute such a statement? But one wonders what manner of person, little or great, seeks a living in this way; is it only to serve a tortured humanity? One wonders.

# 22

The woman lay in her bed, continuing to enjoy its warmth and safety many minutes after her sleep had ended. She stretched her arms out as far as they could go, allowing her legs to sprawl apart at the same time. The bed was comfortable and roomy; it felt quite pleasant stretching out in it. As she lay there, all the world outside was remote and unimportant. The only things real were the bed, her body and the baby inside. It was a delicious few minutes and the woman struggled to make it last as long as possible.

Finally with a puppy-like whimper the woman made herself get up. The day ahead promised to be interminable. It was tiring to think about. She wished it were already evening. She wished that instead of leaving her nice soft bed she were about to enter it. As she washed and dressed, and prepared her breakfast, the woman felt a vague distress at the pleasant feelings that kept bubbling through her body. The image of the gaunt man in the hospital bed flitted through her mind several times but would not stay. Instead of the heaviness and dread of the day before, everything was delicate and wispy. All of her senses were far more sensitive than usual. The silky sensation of warm water splashing on her face, the delightful sting of cold water that left a buzzing in her skin, the clean taste of toothpaste. Everything was good: crunchy toast, pungent hot coffee, the sun breaking through the kitchen window. Everything was good, especially the baby gently floating in her womb.

Several times she tried to grab hold of the flitting image of the man lying in the hospital, but before she could gather it in, it was gone. Little flecks of guilt touched her mind. She was feeling too good and it was not right; there was much to worry about and she was not worrying. She should be sick with grief, but instead she was enjoying an agreeable breakfast. "You should be ashamed of yourself," her mother's words softly whispered through the distance of fifteen years, "eating sweets and enjoying yourself while your poor grandfather lies dead and not yet buried. What sort of girl are you?" The words trailed off and left behind a pressure. "What sort of girl am I?" the woman asked herself, forcing the delightful bubbling sensations to recede. "I should be getting ready to go to the hospital instead of sitting here pretending I haven't got a trouble in the world."

She pushed away the remaining half of her second cup of coffee. "I should be ashamed of myself." As she said the words, in spite of herself a tiny smile flickered at the corner of her mouth—a ray of sunshine lay in her lap and the baby was stirring inside.

The man had been sponged and combed and the room sprayed with aromatic disinfectant just before the woman arrived. He was propped up with an extra pillow and the transfusion needle had been temporarily removed from his arm. It was strange to have both arms free, and the man bent and extended each arm in turn, over and over, trying to drive out the stiffness and ache.

Earlier the resident had been in to listen to his heart and lungs and check his blood pressure. Except for a few terse questions about how he had slept and was there much pain, the doctor had been totally uncommunicative.

The sick man had watched the resident's face while he worked—his intense concentration while listening to the body sounds. Without having any way of confirming his feelings, he was confident that this doctor was a master technician. Anything that could be done, this physician would do. No recent medical advance was unknown to him. Unlike the doctor who had visited him at home, the resident was an expert in his field. The sick man knew all these things and was thankful the resident was assigned to his case; yet at the same time he disliked the doctor. His skin crawled and his muscles tensed at the other's touch. After the doctor left the room, the man thought about his reaction and felt guilty. He had just decided to try to change his feelings, when his wife opened the door.

With scarcely more than a nod of greeting, the man asked in a strong voice, stronger than any the woman had heard him use since the illness began, "Did you have a chance to speak to the resident?"

She shook her head, then sat down using the same chair as the day before. "You sound better, your voice is stronger. You look better," she lied in what she hoped was a natural tone. "How do you feel, honey? You didn't even say hello when I came in."

"Hello," the man mumbled.

"I don't blame you if you're not in a good mood. If you don't feel friendly, you don't have to act—I understand."

"I feel friendly," the man responded hesitantly. "It's just that something bothers me."

"Something I did?" the woman asked softly.

"Yes. I mean no, not something you did, something you didn't do. I just don't understand why you didn't talk to the doctor about what's wrong with me."

"How do you know I didn't?" the woman answered. The annoyance she was beginning to feel crept into her voice.

"I just assumed you didn't."

"I told you I spoke to the resident yesterday morning. It was just before I came in here to your room. I told you he warned me about getting you upset, that it would be the worst thing that could happen."

"He didn't mention anything about my sickness, what I got?"

"He said a few things." The woman was flustered and spoke in a halting fashion. "He was in a hurry and just mentioned one or two things—the same things the other doctor told you . . ."

"Oh." The man let his head fall back on the pillow. His voice diminished until it was scarcely louder than a whisper. "I'm sorry if I was cross with you. I understand."

"That's all right. I'd be cross too if I had to lie all day in that bed. I think you really are acting very nice, considering how much you've been through. Now you have to concentrate on getting well so you can get out of this place and come home where you belong."

"Yes, of course," the man answered. "I must get better so I can come home soon." He looked at his wife and felt a gentle touch of sadness. "You know, baby, even with that gauze mask on, you're pretty, prettier than the day we were married."

The woman wondered what to say. The change in her husband's attitude was so abrupt it left her confused. "Anything I can bring you, anything you need?"

"No, nothing." The man's face relaxed into a gentle smile. "Buy yourself something, a hat, something to cheer you up. You've had a rough time. I mean it. Go get yourself something nice."

Wave after wave of guilt rose up inside the woman as her

husband spoke. "Oh, darling," she sobbed out, hating herself for her lack of concern that morning, "I miss you. I do miss you. I don't want anything except you. Nothing. Oh honey!"

"Now, now," the man lifted his head several inches placing his forefinger on his lips, "don't cry. Don't worry. I'm not worried, see," he smiled, pointing his finger at his face.

The woman stood up, her body quivering. "I'll be back later, I promise." She forced the words through her sobs, then ran out of the room.

The man felt quieter than before. The footfalls, scrapings and voice sounds out in the corridor grew muffled as if the room were filled with invisible cotton. Even the ceiling light grew softer. Although his eyes were open, the man was looking inward and listening, listening to the sounds of his body. For minutes he remained perfectly still, his smile forgotten but still there on his lips. "I wonder how long I have?" The question floated in his mind. "A year, six months, a month? Surely more than a month. Six months, that's it. You always have six months left when they discover you have a fatal disease." The man furrowed his forehead. "I thought I'd feel terrible if I knew. Yesterday I almost panicked. Now I scarcely care. How strange, how very strange. I guess I am braver than I thought. 'Condemned to death and the condemned man was unperturbed!'" A rich languor started filling the man's body. It was as if a dozen transfusion needles were pumping honey mixed with opium into his veins. "I feel so much better," he murmured. "Too bad she's so upset. If she knew how nice and warm I feel, she wouldn't worry." The man's eyes fluttered closed and his breathing grew deep and regular. Several times as he sank deeper and deeper into sleep, he mumbled, "Don't worry, don't worry."

# 23

The main waiting room looked pleasantly familiar as the woman entered. She had decided to spend part of the day in the hospital in spite of her husband's urgings. She noticed that the chair she'd occupied the day before was taken, and unconsciously her face screwed up into the expression of someone who's just smelled a foul odor. A few minutes later the chair became vacant, and the woman scurried across the room and plunked herself into it with a satisfied grunt.

"He sounded a little better, poor thing." The woman reviewed her conversation with her husband. "He sounded stronger and acted as if he felt better, especially at the last."

Her thoughts shifted. She felt the presence of someone close by. She tugged at the hemline of her dress and pressed her thighs tighter together, an action that was more difficult now than before she was pregnant. Her thoughts momentarily returned to her husband. "I must not let myself get so upset. I'm supposed to comfort him, not the other way around."

The man who had been hovering nearby stepped directly in front of her chair. "You sure do look a lot better than when you were in the ambulance." His face was covered with a knowing smirk.

The woman looked at the stranger and raised her eyebrows a little. She did not recognize him, and his open inspection of her face was uncomfortable. "I'm sorry, but I do not think—" She stopped herself in midsentence. She had been fooled by the other's street clothes. "Of course," she beamed, "you were the man in the ambulance. You took care of my husband. I didn't recognize you for a minute. I really am sorry."

"That's OK, no need to apologize. It took me a minute to figure out where I saw you. You certainly do look a lot better than when we brought your husband here." The ambulance attendant's eyes traveled down for a quick inspection of the woman's body, then glanced off to one side. The eye movement was rapid, but it was not lost on the woman. She pushed back into her chair a fraction of an inch.

"How is your husband?" the attendant asked, shifting his eyes back to the woman's face.

"He's a little better today." The woman forced herself to appear at ease.

"Was it an ulcer? I've had my days off, so I never had a chance to ask."

"No." The woman was suddenly very reluctant to answer any more questions. She would have preferred saying nothing, but saw no way to avoid continuing without being rude.

"What did they come up with?" The way the ambulance attendant said "they" expressed the same bitterness he had shown in the ambulance.

"Leukemia, acute leukemia," the woman said, dropping her voice a little.

"Of course, of course. I heard about the case." The attendant tapped his head with his knuckle. "I didn't connect up that case with your husband. I should have known. They mentioned his wife was going to have a baby." He stopped himself, then lowered his voice and shook his head several times. "I'm sorry it was your husband. What a lousy break. Everyone in the hospital is hoping he can . . ." The attendant bit his lower lip, angry at having spoken too much.

"I know, everyone wants him to live until the baby is born. You didn't say anything wrong. I know all the facts." The woman spoke in as controlled a voice as she could muster. The attendant's eyes darting over her body disturbed her, and she began to perspire under her arms.

"If I get a chance today or tomorrow I'll stop in and say hello to your husband. You're a brave woman. I've always admired brave women. If I can do anything . . ." The ambulance attendant reached down and patted the woman's hand allowing his hand to rest on hers for a second. "I'm sure I'll see you again—in the hospital."

As the ambulance attendant walked away, the woman glanced at him from the corner of her eye. She noticed that he was tall and walked loose. "You won't see me again if I can help it." The woman said the words just softly enough that the departing man wouldn't hear them. "He looked me over as if I were a dance hall hostess," she thought. She touched her protruding abdomen. "Seven months pregnant and the way he looked at me—disgusting."

The woman felt a spreading warmth deep inside her body. She clenched her jaws and tried to ignore it for a time. Then she dropped her head, covered her face with her hands, and whispered, "What sort of a woman are you? Your husband is terribly sick and you allow yourself to feel like that." She presssed her thighs together with such force that her muscles started to ache. "Seven months pregnant and he looked at me . . . Oh, God. What will I do, what will I do? If they look at me that way now, what will happen after the baby is born?"

The heat rose up through her body burning the woman's face. "I never want to look at another man. I never will, I never will, I promise. Oh, God. He's lying there so sick, so terribly sick and all I can do is let myself get hot and bothered. I'll never look at another man." Even as the whispered words were coming out of her mouth, somewhere far back in a corner of her mind a tiny thought flickered: "If they look you over now, with your big fat belly sticking out, just wait and see how they react later on. An attractive young widow." The woman struck her head with the palm of her hand. The blow stung and she struck her head a second time with the same degree of force. "Jesus Christ, how do thoughts like that get into my brain? What is the matter with me?"

# 24

The sick man greeted the family doctor with a slight wave of his hand. The doctor had been hesitating at the door, unsure whether the man was still asleep. "Come on in, doc, I'm awake. I slept for a while and I feel better."

The doctor walked in. Before attending to his patient, he adjusted the curtains, letting in a flood of light. "Let's throw some light on the subject; no need keeping this place like a dungeon."

"Thanks, that feels good. It's good to have light. When I'm in my grave, it will be dark enough."

The doctor turned his head and stared at the man. "When you're in your grave?" He forced a deep belly laugh. "That's the way they talk over in geriatrics." He altered his voice so that it sounded old and feeble. "Doc-tor, give me a lit-tle light. It will be dark e-nough in my grave. Oh woe is me."

The sick man chuckled. "I guess I did sound pitiful." He forced his voice in imitation of the doctor's. "These tir-ed old bones make me feel like I'm a hund-red. Must be the rheumatiz."

The doctor sat down on the edge of the bed and chuckled, then bowed his head several times. "You are feeling better. Keep this up and you'll be going home before long."

The man smiled back. He looked directly into the doctor's eyes. "I know I'm going to die." The smile lessened a little, but his eyes remained crinkled. "No need to keep up all the pretending about me getting well and going home. I know what is really going to happen; I can take it."

"Nonsense." The doctor waved his hand disparagingly. "You're worrying yourself needlessly."

"Doctor," the smile vanished from the other's face, "look at me, in my eyes. I know. And I do not want to play any more games. And doctor, I'm not worried."

"Who in the world has been telling you silly things and trying to upset you?" The doctor's face began to turn a deep mottled red.

"Nobody has told me anything. I just know. I understand that you and the others don't want me to be upset. But, doc, look at me, I'm not upset and I know."

The older man looked at the younger carefully. He picked up his patient's hand and held it between both of his for several minutes. "You're a fine young fellow," he finally said in a husky voice. "Let's work hard so you can be on your feet in time for your baby's birth."

"I would like to be around to see the baby," the man said in a soft voice. "You think we have a reasonable chance, doc?"

"Yes." The doctor prolonged the word. "We have a reasonable chance, I think, even a good chance."

"What do I have?"

"Leukemia, a condition of the blood."

"So that's what it is." The man let his breath out slowly. "Leukemia. I knew of a kid in school who had it. His gums were always bleeding. I think he lasted almost a year." The man sighed.

"We didn't want to tell you because we felt it might be easier if you didn't know."

"I understand, doc. I don't blame you for trying to keep me from knowing, but I knew. I knew from the moment I felt that thing inside my stomach. For some, I guess it's better that they don't know. If I have a few months or a year to live, there are things I want to do, lots of little things that need doing. I'm glad we had this talk. I can start making plans."

The doctor watched the sick man's face as he spoke, nodding his head every few seconds. When the man paused to catch his breath, the doctor said, "There are differences of opinion among physicians. I personally feel that making plans is always a good idea if the patient can handle it. In your case, you can handle it."

"I can handle it." The man sighed again. "So, you think I have a good chance to see my baby born?"

"No question about it. You're feeling better today. You sound better. These are very encouraging signs. If you can avoid picking up a bug . . . with a little luck, not too much, just a little . . . no point in my saying any more, you understand." The older man stood up still holding his patient's hand. "I'm an old-fashioned doctor and there is a devil of a lot I don't know, but one thing I do know is that the patient plays a damn important role in affecting the course of his illness."

"I understand." The man squeezed the doctor's hand. "I'll do my part."

As soon as the doctor was out of the room, the man turned his head toward the sunlight shimmering through the window. He opened his eyes very wide and stared at the brightness, forcing himself not to blink. After a few minutes, his eyes began to water. He tried to hold them open a little longer, but the stinging finally caused them to close involuntarily. Some of the brightness remained after they were closed, waves of warm light that washed deep into his brain. Finally the pulsing light grew dim, leaving behind a chill that turned colder and colder.

"Why did it have to happen to me?" the man whispered. "Why do some people get these things and others don't? I was sure it was something fatal, something terrible, but there was a tiny little bit of doubt until now." The man felt tears forming under his closed eyelids. "I sounded so big and brave talking to the doctor. I knew, but somehow I expected to find out that I was wrong. Deep down inside I expected that after all the worrying, I would find out that I'd be all right. Like a dream—you finally wake up."

The man's thoughts slid away as he sank into a state that was midway between sleeping and waking. It was a special state that in the past had come on those rare occasions when he found himself thoroughly exhausted but unable to rest. It was a condition where dreams and memories and real events got mixed up together, where he wasn't sure if he were dreaming or thinking.

The man was a little boy and he lay on his bed clutching a model boat his father had helped him build. He heard people talking in the other room—they were saying, "Shall we tell him?" It was dark and he knew that his father lay dead in the other room. Suddenly it was silent—terribly silent. The voices had gone and instead of a boat, he held a toy gun. No one was in the house except the dead man. His mother had gone. Everyone was gone. The toy gun wasn't a toy; it was real and heavy and somehow he had accidentally shot and killed his father. There were sirens and he wanted to hide under the bed, but was afraid of what he might find there. He heard them carrying something down the stairs and wondered if it was his father or the old man, Tannenbaum. "I killed him, I killed him," he started shouting. He was afraid they would hear him, but he couldn't help shouting. "Oh why did I do it? I didn't mean to." Tears ran down his face. He fought against the terrible dream and woke up and found himself lying in his bed. He heard his mother fixing breakfast and the sounds

111

of his father getting ready in the bathroom. He cried. It felt so good to know it had been a dream and he hadn't killed his father.

The man struggled to bring himself up out of the halfway state; as soon as he was completely awake, he would find that it had all been an ugly dream, like the one about his father. He tugged and pulled at his mind, trying to bring himself to wakefulness. His eyes wouldn't open. He felt himself sinking down. "If I don't wake up, I will die," he told himself. "I have to wake up so that I'll find it all isn't true. It all has been a dream, a horrible dream—I'm really home in my bed. It all has been a dream like the one about my father. I must get my eyes open. I must wake up." He struggled and pushed with all the strength that was in him. "I must get awake and find it isn't so. If I can only move one finger, one little finger, I can wake up." He concentrated all his being on moving one finger and the finger moved.

The man sprang into total consciousness; his eyes flew open. For a moment he was dazzled by the sunlight falling on his face. He moved his head until he could see, then let out a gasp. "Oh no, it's real. Oh God, I wasn't dreaming. It's real." He swung his arms out, striking the metal bedguards as a flood of crying poured out of his body. "I thought when I awoke it would be gone like that other time. Why does it have to be real? Why can't it be a dream? Oh God, please make it a dream."

Suddenly the man bit down on his lower lip until it stung. He held his mouth closed trying to stop the crying. "I hope nobody heard me. I'm crying like a baby. It's all true, so you might as well accept it. Blubbering and going to pieces won't do you any good. If your wife sees you this way, it will only make things worse." The man kept his lip between his teeth until the crying spasms had been reduced to an occasional shudder. He wiped his face carefully with the edge of the sheet, then husbanding his energy adjusted himself in the bed and lay perfectly still.

The man lay on the bed with his eyes half closed, his face free of expression. Carefully, he reviewed the situation. "The only difference between me and anyone else is that instead of dying in twenty or thirty or forty years, my time will be up in months. Most people don't go walking around worrying about when they are going to die, so there's no reason why I should. The only difference between me and others is the length of time. Everybody has to go. It's only a question of when. I can either accept what is going to happen and enjoy the next few months or I can become upset and lose the enjoyment. Either way I can't stop what will happen from happening. I'll get myself on my feet—enjoy each day as much as I can, be around when my baby is born, see how it feels to be a father. Then when my time is up, when I feel it coming, that will be time enough to start worrying." The man was comforted by his thoughts as he lay there. Every time he felt the beginnings of an icy twinge inside his chest, he murmured to himself, "I can either enjoy the next few months or get upset and lose the enjoyment." Each time, the words caused the icy sensation to recede and allowed him a few minutes of peace.

# 25

The man was deeply engrossed in thought when his wife entered the room. During most of the afternoon he had fallen asleep for a few minutes at a time, but had been unable to stay asleep. In the midst of his thinking he would drift off, then suddenly snap awake and continue with the same thought as if there had been no interruption. He nodded to the woman and smiled a little, but would have preferred that she wait a while longer before coming in.

"You don't look like you're too happy to see me." The woman spoke in a half-serious, half-joking manner. "If you want me to come back later, that's OK. I can go eat something, then come back."

"No," the man lifted himself partway up on one elbow, "it's all right. I was thinking and I didn't expect you just yet."

"I didn't go shopping like you said. I sat downstairs in the waiting room, then went for a walk, but I didn't go shopping."

"You don't have to stay around the hospital all day, honey." The man spoke tenderly. "I want you to take care of yourself. You don't have to visit twice a day. I'm better."

"I want to visit twice a day." The woman answered in an almost angry voice. "You are my husband and I want to visit as often as I'm allowed."

"All right, all right," the man chuckled, settling back in his bed. "Don't bite my head off."

"I'm sorry, I didn't mean to sound gruff. If the situations were reversed, I know that you would visit as often as possible. What kind of a wife do you think I am?"

"A darn nice wife. Too bad I'm laid up here in the hospital. If we were home I'd show you what kind of a wife I think you are." As he spoke, the man tried to make his voice sound as suggestive as possible.

"You are getting better," the woman giggled. "All those young nurses running around the hospital better watch their step."

"Ugh, double-ugh," the man winked one eye slowly, "except for the night nurse. That nurse and I have had some interesting conversations."

Almost as a reflex, the woman responded defensively. "If you want to flirt, it doesn't bother me one single bit." For a moment the reality of the situation vanished and she felt hurt. "Is she very pretty?"

"Don't tell me you're jealous?" the man asked, feigning surprise.

"Not a bit, not even a tiny bit." The woman began to realize how inappropriate her reaction had been and attempted to join in the banter, although she still was not completely at ease. "You both will probably end up having a mad affair."

"I doubt that, I seriously doubt that."

"I thought you said she was pretty."

"I said nothing of the sort. To tell the truth," the man paused, stroking his chin with a grossly exaggerated gesture, "she is not pretty. In fact, she is not even a she; she's a he." He began to chuckle, but the chuckle quickly faded as he grew short of breath.

"A he, a male nurse!" The woman laughed harder than she had to. "I was beginning to get jealous, I'll confess. I was getting pretty mad. A male nurse. Maybe I don't know what I'm missing by not being in the hospital."

"Now wait a minute." The man, still short of breath, was forced to speak slowly between gulps of air. "As long as I'm around, there is only one man in your life, understand."

"I promise." The woman raised her right hand in the sign of a pledge. "You are the only man I'll ever want. There will never be anyone else." Each word was carefully enunciated and she kept her hand raised until she had finished speaking.

The man looked at his wife. Her mouth and nose were hidden by the gauze mask, but her eyes were not and they glistened as if they were ready to weep. "That was very nice of you to say." He still spoke slowly, but in a huskier voice. "Never is a long time."

"I don't care, I meant every word of it." Tears started spilling out of the woman's eyes.

The man turned his head away toward the window. He adjusted his arm and his pillow so that his wife would be unable to see his face. "You are a good brave woman." The huskiness in his voice grew more pronounced. "And you are a good wife, but never is a long time. Honey, I know what's wrong with me. I know I don't have very long to live, so let's stop kidding each other."

"You'll probably outlive me and all the doctors." The woman shook off her crying and tried to sound cheerful. "You start worrying and you convince yourself that you are sicker than you really are."

The man spoke softly. "I know I have leukemia."

The woman sucked in her breath and began twisting her hands together. "So you know." Her voice was flat. "So they finally told you."

"I knew all along there was something terribly wrong. I didn't know exactly what it was, but I knew I wasn't going to

116

live. I had a talk with the doctor this morning and he told me."

"The resident didn't want me to say anything." The woman's voice was completely expressionless and her face had lost all of its pinkish color.

"It wasn't the resident, it was the other doctor, the one who came to the house."

"Are you upset?" The woman felt herself growing frightened as she asked the question. She had an urge to jump up and run out of the room.

"Am I upset? No, not really. Well, maybe a little. It's all so strange. It's hard to believe."

The woman's heart began to pound rapidly and she felt a pressure in her head; the urge to leave the room was almost uncontrollable. "Maybe," her mouth was dry and she found it difficult to speak, "it would be better if you didn't talk about it, didn't think about it."

"I want to talk about it," the man burst out.

The woman stumbled to her feet. "I gotta go to the toilet," she mumbled. Without waiting for a response, she ran out of the room.

The man let his eyes close while he waited for his wife to return. He hadn't noticed anything unusual about her behavior. Most of his attention had been directed inward and his only reaction to her sudden exit was a vague thought that her pregnant condition was to blame for the physical emergency.

The woman leaned over the washbasin in the ladies' room scooping up handfuls of cold water, splashing them in her face. Some of the water ran down her neck, wetting the front of her dress. She looked into the mirror over the basin and said out loud, "I can't go back in there. I can't go back. I can't talk to him about dying. If I go back, I'll faint." She lowered her head until her face was under the stinging cold water and forced herself to stay in that position until her lungs felt as if

117

they were about to burst. "What is the matter with me?" she blubbered into the water. "I'm not going to die, I don't have leukemia. What am I so afraid of?"

She lifted her head and shook it rapidly from side to side. "I felt as if I was the one that was dying. When he started talking, it was me. I don't know what came over me." She stared in the mirror, looking directly into her own eyes. "You cut that out," she hissed at herself. "You just quit it. He is the sick one, not you. Now you just cut that out." With slow and deliberate movements the woman blotted her face dry, dried the washbowl and rearranged her disordered hair. Just before leaving she turned back to the mirror; her eyes were angry and her forehead deeply furrowed. "The one time someone really needs you, and you go to pieces. You should be ashamed!"

As she reentered the room, the woman tightened her jaw and forced herself to stand unnaturally straight, maintaining her body rigidity even after she had resumed her seat.

"Are you OK? You were gone so long I was beginning to worry."

"I'm sorry, I stopped to fix my hair." The woman controlled her voice, keeping it down in her throat so that it sounded almost masculine. "You must not worry about me. I'm sorry I left while you were talking, but I'm back now, so please continue."

"You sound funny." The man turned his head until he was looking directly at her. "Is there anything wrong?"

The woman shook her head several times.

"I was thinking while you were gone," the man continued, "that it's lucky I have someone like you to talk to. Someone who understands. And another thing," he lowered his eyes, embarrassed for the moment, "I'm glad we are going to have a baby. I think I'm happier about that than anything else in the world."

"I'm glad I am going to have your baby." The stiffness went out of the woman as she relaxed in her seat. "I want more than anything else to have you with me when I'm having it."

"Don't worry," the man's voice vibrated with confidence, "I'll be with you. This stinking disease may be fatal—but before it gets me, it will have a fight on its hands. This old walrus is not about to throw in the towel. I'll be with you when the baby comes and for some months afterwards; you can count on it."

"Of course you will, I know you will." She paused, then continued. "All over the world they're working, trying to find a cure for it. Maybe they're on the verge right now. Maybe in a few weeks or a few months they'll have the answer."

The man's eyes started to glisten. "That's a pretty long shot, one in a million, but you never know. You even hear of cases, cases where all the doctors say there isn't a chance and the patient outlives the doctor."

"I know, honey, you read about it in the papers all the time. I once heard of a man who was dying of cancer; his body was filled with it, and all of a sudden it was gone. They gave him X-rays and everything and it was all gone."

The man smiled weakly. He was breathing rapidly again, but tried to ignore his growing exhaustion. "Those cases happen one in ten thousand, one in a hundred thousand. Maybe I'll be the lucky one, but I doubt it. It's really silly to even talk about it. When those things happen, they are miracles and I'm not expecting any miracles."

The woman stood up and walked over to the bed. "The first thing is for you to be with me when the baby comes. After that we can think about the next thing."

The man's voice softened to a whisper as he felt himself about to sink into sleep. "No matter what happens," he said, "even if I don't last long enough to see it, some of me will

119

still be living. This stinking place can't take that away from me."

After the man had fallen asleep the woman started to leave, then turned back. Her head twitched several times as she looked at his face. "You poor baby, why did it have to happen to you?" She felt a dull pressure tugging at the organs in her chest. "I wonder if what I said to that fat woman really was right?" she asked herself. "I wonder if I did have something to do with his getting sick. When I first had that thought I didn't know how bad he was. Maybe the whole idea is foolish. How could I make him sick? Even if I had a part in it, it's everything, it's not just me, it's all the rottenness in the world —all the bad things work their way into the marrow of your bones." The woman raised her head with a strange look of wonder on her face. "Into the marrow of your bones, like leukemia."

# 26

Several times during the evening the nurse entered the room to replace the transfusion bottle and check on the man's condition. These movements in and out did not disturb the man; even detaching the empty bottle and connecting the full one was not enough to interrupt his regular breathing. But a few minutes before midnight a gust of rain whipped against the window, and he was startled into wakefulness.

The room was dark. The door to the corridor had been closed and only the tiniest sliver of light shone through the crack at its base. A second burst of raindrops rattled the window and the man turned in the direction of the sound. Outside the wind twisted and nagged at the window until a coil of cold air worked its way into the room. The sounds of the storm and the sensation of the chilled air touching his face and hands were strangely satisfying. He thought for a moment about going to the window and forcing it open and letting great gusts of rain beat against his face and chest. He wanted to suck in lungfuls of cold storm-washed air, to open his mouth and feel the wind rushing down his throat and the raw raindrops on his tongue. He reached out and gripped the cold metal bedguard and for several seconds wondered if he had the strength to get out of his bed. He pulled himself up several inches, then let go and fell backwards with a gasp. A tearing pain traveled up his arm and into his shoulder.

He lay perfectly still for a few minutes until the pain receded, then turned his attention back to the storm outside. "Too bad it's winter. It would be good to see lightning." The man talked to himself in a soft voice. He was not aware that he was speaking. "Lightning and thunder, baroom boom boom, thunder and wild streaks of light in the sky. I wouldn't be a bit upset to be lying on the ground with bolts of lightning sizzling and cracking all around me. Knowing you are going to die has one advantage. Things like lightning can't scare you." He tried to bring back an image of a sky torn open with jagged streaks of summer lightning. "I could actually enjoy watching it instead of being afraid that I might be struck."

Ever since his childhood he had been uneasy during lightning storms. The danger of standing out in the open or hiding under a tree during an electrical storm had been explained to him and he always took the necessary precautions. Yet in spite of his precautions, even when he lay safe in his bed, the blue white flashes caused his heart to beat rapidly and his hands to perspire.

"What a way to go," the man's pulse began to race, "out under the sky with the rain and the wind, then boom!—struck right through the middle—dead before you know it." The spoken words stopped, but the thoughts continued. "Better than oozing away drop by drop. Bang, it's all over. This way it's just down, down, like sinking slowly into a cesspool until your head finally goes under.

"When I get back on my feet," the thoughts turned back into spoken words, "after the baby is born, after I do everything that needs to be done. When I start to feel myself slipping, then boom! I'll make it happen quick." The man raised his hand in the dark holding it in the sign of an oath. He had grown aware that he was speaking out loud and allowed his voice to rise until it was almost at conversational level. "I will not let myself die an inch at a time. After the baby, when I feel it coming, I'll make it quick. I hereby swear to God that before I let them take me back to this place, I'll do whatever has to be done."

The man dropped his arm. His breathing was very rapid and his heart felt as if it were beating inside his throat. "I'm so weak," he murmured, "the least little thing makes me feel like I'm gonna pass out. I'll be glad when this part is over. Christ, I want to get out of this place and have my strength back, even for a little while." He shifted his body several inches trying to find a more comfortable position. The ache in his arms and legs was dull, much less than at first, but he could not completely ignore it. No matter where his thoughts might wander, the feeling in his arms and legs finally dragged his mind back to himself. Lying there, still short of breath, he thought about his bones and wondered what they were like inside. He tried to experience his bones as separate and distinct from his legs and arms. He concentrated intensely trying to feel inside his body and as he was concentrating, he suddenly became aware of the feeling of the air on his skin, the sensation of his body pressing against the bed and the bed pressing back against his body. Things he had never noticed now absorbed his entire attention: the change in the temperature of the air as it moved into his nose, down the back of his throat and into his lungs; the sound of blood pulsing through the arteries in his ears; the passage of food out of his stomach into the small intestine. So much was happening inside his body that he'd never noticed before.

As the man lay on the bed more aware of his body than at any other time in his life, a delicious sensation washed over him. It was as if he had suddenly been placed in a bath of sweet warm oil. For several moments he felt a weightlessness as his body floated in this imaginary oil. "Life is good," the sick man whispered. "It's a shame we have to die."

The weightlessness faded, but the man still was encased in a cocoon of contentment. "If I could feel like this," he thought, "I wouldn't care about dying. If I could only feel like this, nothing would matter."

The wind beat against the window and rain hissed and spattered. Outside in the corridor occasional soft footfalls came and went. The seconds and minutes moved by. Still, the man glowed with the sensations of living.

"I'm well." The thought floated up like a curl of smoke. "I feel nothing—no pain—nothing. I'm well." The thought brought with it a gush of delight, and warm tears started rolling down his cheeks. Without moving a muscle he focused his mind as if it were a beam of light on each of his arms and legs. Each limb was carefully examined, toes and fingers, knees and elbows, hips and shoulders. There was no pain. The ache, the deep bone cold, the strange numbness, the prickling, were all gone. He turned his mind to the rest of his body and probed for pain in his chest and abdomen, in his throat and head. There was none. The delight was like a stream of perfumed bubbles. Something had happened, he did not want to think what, something fantastic—a miracle.

"You're well, you can get up, you can get up and get dressed and go home." Tears of gratitude ran out of the corners of his eyes and splashed on the pillow next to his ears. He continued to lie motionless, not allowing so much as his little finger to move. "You can get up." The thought filled his mind so that there was no room for anything else. "Get up, get up."

Slowly the man reached out and gripped the sides of his bed, then using all his strength he gave a mighty tug. He felt himself moving; his arms tightened and he was almost sitting straight up when a flaming jet of pain raced down each arm setting fire to his entire body. The pain was so intense he couldn't catch his breath; yet for a second he refused to let go of the metal bars. He pulled himself up another inch, then his hands went dead and he tumbled backwards.

"No, no," he moaned, "I'm well, I must get up, I'm well." The fire tore at his skin, gnawing deeper and deeper into his flesh. Inside his abdomen he felt a horribly familiar sensation. "I woke it up," he gasped. "No, no, please stop. I woke it up, it's going to tear my guts to pieces." The man's mouth opened wide and he started screaming, "Get it out of me, get it out of me!"

When the nurse snapped on the light, he saw the man's eyes shifting wildly from side to side while his hands clawed at his abdomen.

"He said he wanted to get out of bed," the nurse whispered to the intern who had been aroused from a short nap and was still red-eyed. "He said he wanted to go home because he was well and he wanted to taste the raindrops. The poor kid." The nurse shrugged his shoulder. "I don't know what got into him. He was quiet for hours. I checked on him and he was sleeping, then he tries to get out of bed. I gave him a hypo and he kept murmuring about a mouse in his belly. The poor kid."

The intern felt the unconscious man's pulse. "Good thing you calmed him down. A little more and he might have started hemorrhaging again. He's a very sick boy. Better keep him restrained for the next few days. It would be a damn shame if he lost his chance to be around when the baby is born because we weren't careful. I wonder what he was thinking of, trying to get up. I wonder what kind of crazy nonsense was running through his mind."

# 27

The storm beating on the bedroom window woke the woman up. Without thinking she turned to her husband's side of the bed, seeking comfort. The sheets were cold; there was no warm body to push against. The woman pulled back. The cold empty space made her feel lonely. Outside the wind banged against the building and in the next room a window shade was flapping. The rooms were terribly dark and the whole world felt empty.

"I wonder if they ever let a wife stay with her husband in the hospital?" she asked herself. "Put another bed in the room—it would be nice for both of them. I wonder if there is any place in the world where they do that. It would be nice if a mother were allowed to be with her child." The woman tucked the blankets more securely around her shoulders and nuzzled her face deeper into the pillow. "I wish he was home," she sighed. "These last three days have twisted me all around so I don't know what is going on inside my head half the time." She burrowed a little further into the bed, then pulled her legs up until her thighs rested against her swollen abdomen. "The whole thing is so confused I don't know what to believe. I still can't believe that you're well one day, and the next . . ." Her thoughts trailed off. "I only saw one dead person in my life, my grandfather, and he was old."

The woman allowed her mind to drift back through the years. The wildly flapping window shade reminded her of the insistent knocking on the front door the night her grandfather died. She lay asleep and woke up when someone pounded at the door. All the lights in the house were out and everyone was in bed. Nothing like this had ever happened before. She heard her parents' bedroom door open and her father's heavy steps as he went downstairs. His angry voice as he shouted through the bolted door reverberated through the house, bringing her mother out onto the upper landing. Then came the sounds of the door chain being unhooked and the lock turned, whispers too faint to be heard, several people entering. She heard her mother running downstairs, gasping and crying. The lights in the living room and kitchen went on and there was a constant murmur of voices. It was still dark night outside, yet her house was filled with sounds and with people. She eased out of bed and tiptoed downstairs. Somehow she felt she was doing something naughty. There were relatives in the living room and her mother sat on the couch hugging another woman. Both were crying. Someone was boiling coffee in the kitchen and several plates of fruit and candy had been laid out and were being emptied. She crept close to the door wondering if she would have a chance to sneak a piece of candy before she was caught and sent back to bed. Instead of punishment, the moment she was observed she was snatched up and hugged and kissed. One after another the relatives fondled her, and within a minute her mouth was stuffed with candy and her cheek pocked with lipstick. She was even offered a cup of coffee, something that had never happened before in her life. It was not good, but she drank it and felt important and safe. Nothing she might do would bring punishment; there was no limit to the amount of candy she could eat. Her mother's eyes remained closed as she rocked back and forth in the arms of an older woman; her father stayed in the kitchen whispering with some other men. Everybody was careful not to talk about her grandfather while she could hear, but she already had overheard before entering the room. She knew her grandfather was dead but somehow did not connect this fact with the pleasant old man who took her for walks and gave her dimes and quarters. 'Dead' was a bad word, almost a naughty word, but like all the other bad words it really had no meaning to her. She fell asleep in the living room and in the morning stayed in bed as late as she wanted —she didn't have to go to school. Different adults played with her all through the day.

Thinking about her grandfather's death brought back the excitement of that time. There were moments of sadness, and she dutifully cried when it was expected of her and allowed herself to be comforted when that was expected; but most of all it was exciting, and the stiff neatly dressed man with make-up on his face looked much more like a large doll than like her grandfather.

Without any warning her thoughts shifted from her grandfather to her husband. "I wonder what it will be like when he is dead." An image of her husband dressed in a dark suit with his eyes closed and make-up on his face flashed before her eyes. For a fraction of a second the excitement and fun of her grandfather's death was transferred to the vision of her husband. The picture and the feelings were ripped away as the woman threw off her covers and pushed herself out of bed. She stood trembling in the night chill.

"I must be crazy," she moaned, "too much upset. I'm just not in my right mind." She was comforted by this excuse. No other explanation could have met her need at that moment. "I'll take it easy tomorrow. All that pressure and the baby taking its share of my energy. I'm just not thinking normally. No reason for me to be angry at myself."

She shuddered as the cold worked its way into her body,

tightening her skin and raising thousands of tiny goose pimples. Without putting on her bathrobe or slippers, still trembling from the cold, she forced herself to walk in the dark into the next room. She adjusted the flapping window shade, then still in the dark went through the apartment checking each window. Her penance over, she returned to bed. Although vaguely feeling that she owed her husband several minutes of wifely thought, she was unable to remain awake and slid off to sleep, both arms hugging her stomach.

# 28

In the hospital dining room a handful of staff, night-shift workers, were drinking coffee. The male nurse sat with his eyes partially closed. His body sagged over the table and his forehead almost touched the edge of his coffee cup. His shift was half over; the remaining half was exhausting to think about. "I don't need any more problems on my shift," he grumbled into the cup. "Let the day nurse have her share. Everything always happens at night."

"Talking to yourself?"

The male nurse looked up into the tight-lipped face of the nurse who worked in the emergency room. She stood over the table waiting to be asked to sit down and he nodded her into a seat. "Why do all the worst problems take place during the night? Things can be normal all day, then as soon as the night shift takes over, wham!"

"Having a difficult time tonight?" The angular-faced woman showed by her expression that she understood what the other was saying.

"One of my patients, an old crock, is terminal. He looked like he might last another few days. Now I doubt if he'll make it till morning. And I have this leukemia patient—he suddenly decided he was cured and tried to get out of bed.

Thank God I had the bedguard up or no telling what might have happened. Poor kid wanted to go home and be with his wife."

"I know the case." The emergency room nurse made a clucking sound with her tongue. "We had him when he came in. We worked on him for a couple of hours. His wife is pregnent, seven months, I think."

"Yeah, that's the one. We put him in intensive care, Room 208."

"How is he doing? Do they think he'll last the two months?"

"Who knows? The resident is very interested in the case. I guess everybody is pulling for him. I suppose it's about fifty-fifty, but can you imagine, he tried to get out of bed. Most of the time he's so weak we have to feed him."

"I find the best thing is to be firm." The emergency room nurse looked at her colleague in such a way it appeared she was accusing him of being lax. "It's too easy to spoil patients like that. Everyone is constantly making a big fuss and it ends up creating problems for all the staff. Even I had the tendency in the past to be too lenient with the young incurables. In the long run, it's better when they are treated like all the rest."

"I doubt if he really knew what he was doing," the male nurse answered defensively.

"That may very well be, but it has been my experience if they know the rules and know that the rules will be enforced, even when they are delirious or agitated, there is some control. I'm not saying in every case; there are always exceptions."

"What an old bitch," the male nurse thought. "Tough as elephant hide, but she's a good nurse. Maybe I am a little too easygoing." Then he said out loud, "The intern came up and ordered the patient restrained for the next couple of days. That should help him get the message."

The emergency room nurse got up and carefully smoothed

out her uniform. She nodded her head and said crisply, "I am convinced that most patients do better if you treat them as if they were children. That way they have nothing to worry about; they don't have to make any upsetting decisions and the hospital runs far more efficiently. It is up to the nurse," she stressed the word nurse, "all of us, to set the tone for the hospital. Often the easy way is the hard way in the long run."

"Maybe you're right." The male nurse felt guilty but was not quite sure of what. "But I'm convinced no matter what anyone told him, that kid would have tried to get out of bed. Even if you had been on the floor, I'll bet it would have happened."

With a noticeable snort, the emergency room nurse wheeled around and walked away, muttering in a voice loud enough for the other to hear, "And he calls himself a nurse. Humph!"

All during the two-minute walk back to the emergency room, she continued to mutter. "He can be sure that if I had been on duty, it would have been a different story. Ninety percent of those so-called accidents can be avoided if the nurse remains alert and strictly enforces the rules. A hospital is not a place for people to enjoy themselves. Lots of patients have been grateful because I insisted that the rules be obeyed. Humph!" She snorted again, then blew her nose with a loud trumpeting sound. Her monologue had the effect of heightening her annoyance, and as she walked her eyes darted in every direction looking for a suitable target for her vexation. "If he had been up checking his patients instead of sitting on his lard-filled butt, nothing would have happened. The idea of telling me that it wouldn't have made any difference if I had been on duty. I take care of my patients, not like a lot that I could mention."

As soon as she entered the emergency room, the nurse confronted the intern with her indignation. "You remember

132

that leukemia patient, the one with the wife. Well, I understand he tried to get out of bed."

"Yes, I know. I was called up. The nurse was afraid he was going to hemorrhage. I gave him some sedation. The poor kid thought he had been cured and wanted to go home." The intern started cracking his knuckles one by one, oblivious to the slight shudder that went through the woman each time the bones popped.

"Don't you think if the nurse had been more vigilant, the whole problem would have been avoided?" The nurse had sucked in her cheeks so that her face had become hatchet-shaped. She looked at the young doctor with eyes narrowed down to tiny slits.

"The patient didn't actually get out of bed—thank God. I don't see how the nurse was at fault."

"Don't you think that if the hospital rules were more rigidly enforced, if all the staff," the nurse almost shouted the word 'all,' "did their jobs properly, these so-called accidents could be avoided?"

The intern suddenly noticed the nurse's face. Her lips were a bluish white and her entire body quivered. He reacted with the care of a man who awakens and finds a poisonous snake curled in his lap. "Of course," the intern quickly reviewed what the nurse had just said, "most accidents could be avoided. If everyone were conscientious, as conscientious as a dedicated few," the words had to be forced and they sounded hollow to his ears. "If everyone were conscientious, there would be very few accidents."

"If I had been on duty, I can assure you that patient would not have tried to get out of bed. I keep close check on my patients and I make sure they know the rules." The nurse stopped speaking and looked at the intern for confirmation.

The young doctor was acutely uncomfortable. Somehow, he didn't know how, his entire future relationship with this woman depended upon what he said now. Despite his medical rank, he was afraid of the nurse, afraid of what she could do to him, to his career. "If the patient had been more carefully watched, it would not have happened." The intern quickly glanced at the other's face to see if he had said enough. "If you had been on duty, I'm sure you would have kept close check on the patient."

The nurse nodded her head with considerable force. "Those of us who do our job have a responsibility to make sure that the rest are forced to do theirs, don't you agree, doctor?"

The intern grunted in the affirmative. He knew by the woman's use of the word "us" he was now considered an ally. He turned around and pretended to be occupied with a medical report. For several minutes he continued to hold the papers in front of his face. He felt like a weak silly little boy who was playing at the game of doctor. When the nurse finally walked out of the room, he turned back to make sure she was gone, then stuck his middle finger up into the air.

# 29

The male nurse peeked into the man's room as soon as he returned to his duty station. The sick man moved restlessly in bed and moaned softly. The nurse turned on the light and walked in. The patient's eyes were wide open, the pupils dilated, and he appeared to be staring at something far away. "What's the matter, fellow?" the nurse asked gently as he adjusted the patient's pillow. "Everything is all right. Go back to sleep. You don't have anything to worry about."

"Don't want to be tied down." The man's words were thick and he spoke slowly and with great effort.

"It's for your own good." The nurse tested the straps, making sure that they were buckled securely. "We all want you to get well and we don't want to take any chances. You tried to get out of bed before, remember?"

"I'm not an animal." The man pushed his body feebly against the straps. "I'm gonna die anyhow, so why tie me up?"

"You are not going to die. You're going to get well. Now just put all those bad thoughts out of your mind and go to sleep like a good boy."

"I'm no baby. Don't treat me like a baby." The sick man began to cry. "Don't tie me up. I know I got leukemia. Don't tell me I'm gonna be well."

*the dance*

The nurse pulled back several inches, muttering between his teeth, "Who the hell told him? Bunch of damn fools." Then he leaned over the patient and checked the transfusion needle. "The doctor gave you some medicine to make you sleep. If you stop fighting it, you'll fall asleep and feel much better in the morning."

"I promise I won't try and get up. If you take off these straps, I swear I won't even lift one hand. Please. I can't stand to be tied down."

"I'm sorry, pal. Doctor's orders. If you behave for the next day or two, I'm sure he'll take them off, but you might as well go to sleep because there is nothing that can be done now."

"Am I an animal?" The sick man's words had grown so thick that they sounded like those of an habitual drunk. "Only animals are tied up. Let me go, let me go." He raised his voice until it was almost a shout.

"Now you listen." The nurse leaned all the way over the bed and looked directly into his patient's eyes. The words of the emergency room nurse still nettled his mind. "I don't want any more fussing tonight, do you understand? You are not the only patient in the hospital. Now go to sleep."

The sick man's eyes opened wider. Tears kept flowing down his cheeks. "I'm afraid," he whispered. "Don't leave me alone. Don't leave me here in the dark."

The nurse straightened up and hesitated several seconds. "I'll leave the light on if you promise to go to sleep." The patient nodded his head. "I will be back to check on you in fifteen or twenty minutes and I expect to find you fast asleep when I return." The patient nodded again. "Now close your eyes!" The patient dutifully allowed his lids to close. "Don't forget. I expect to find you fast asleep when I return."

The sick man continued to keep his eyes closed after the

nurse left the room. He was thankful for the light, a portion of which filtered through his lids. He was groggy and his mind swam in a pool of thoughts and feelings. He tried to ignore the restraining straps; he tried to ignore the tiny ice darts of fear that kept burrowing into his chest. He repeated to himself the nurse's warning that he was expected to be fast asleep in fifteen minutes.

The nurse's words brought back bits of a scene that had taken place years earlier. He was in kindergarten and sat on a little chair in front of a little table. It was quiet time and his head lay on the table. Every so often the teacher would speak to one or another of the children about their head not being still or their eyes not being closed. He remembered how hard it was to remain quiet and to keep his eyes closed when there was so much to see. That day, at the end of quiet time, the teacher told the class that summer vacation was about to start and that all the boys and girls would be expected to know the alphabet when they entered the first grade in the fall. All during the summer he was worried that he would not be able to learn it. The thought of returning to school without knowing the letters kept him uneasy and afraid much of the time.

The nurse's order, to be asleep in fifteen minutes, felt like the teacher's order given years earlier. The man was afraid that the nurse would return and find him still awake. Just as with the kindergarten teacher, he did not think about what would happen if he were not asleep. It was not fear of punishment, rather it was the idea of being disobedient. If he did not obey, he would not be loved. He was weak and vulnerable and terrified of anyone not loving him.

The nurse did not return in fifteen minutes as he had promised. An hour had passed and the patient was in a deep sleep when the nurse stuck his head in the door. He switched off the light and waited a moment. The patient's breathing continued deep and regular. "I hated to talk to him like that," the nurse apologized to himself as he carefully closed the door, "but if I hadn't been firm, he might have fussed all night and made himself sicker. Too bad he knows what's wrong. It's going to make him a lot harder to manage."

# 30

Despite the drugs, despite his exertions, despite the enormous drain on his emotions, the man was unable to remain asleep. Not so much as a trace of light filtered through the curtains. The man had no clue as to the time. He was unable to judge whether he had slept several hours or several minutes. He had learned that how he felt physically was no longer a reliable indication. His body had become a giant rubber doll filled with wet sawdust and broken glass. Not a single part of his body felt as it had before the sickness. Even the slightest movement required conscious effort. Often the effort was more distressing than the need to move.

The restraining straps reduced considerably the decisions the sick man had to make. He could not shift position; thus he did not have to weigh the expenditure of energy and the sharp muscular pains of moving against the deep aches and numbness of lying still. He remembered, as if it had happened a long time ago, his distress at being strapped down and his pleading tears. He wondered why he had been so upset. Being strapped down was a condition of existence. It seemed like he had been restrained since before he could remember.

He thought for a moment about dying, but thinking of death was not important. It was a waste of time. Anything that might happen the next day or next month or next year was a vast distance away. The only important things were those in this moment and the next. A cold drink of water was far more valuable than a promise that his life would last so many months or days or years. He considered calling out for a glass of water, but the water was less valuable than the energy needed to call out. Sooner or later someone would come and bring him water.

The man decided to take inventory of what he could do. The first thing that came to his mind and made him tingle with excitement was the realization that he could think—anything he wanted. He could think forward or backward or out to either side. The number of thoughts possible was so great it frightened him. "I could go on for a thousand years and never use them up," he told himself, "like the loaf of bread that never grew less."

Then he began to consider all the physical things that were possible. It took him several minutes to realize how wide a selection was available. At first all he could discover were the obvious ones—the movement of his fingers and toes. Then he found that he could turn his feet in either direction, clench or unclench his hands, rotate his arms, shrug his shoulders, move his head from side to side, lift his head several inches, push it deeper into the pillow and do an incredible number of combinations of movements to say nothing of tightening and untightening a bewildering number of muscles.

"Facial expression," he thought, "anything I want. Laugh, cry, frown, smile, make a monkey face, stick my tongue out." The man bubbled with excitement. "I can swallow. I think I can belch, maybe fart. How about breathing? I breathe fast or slow, deep or shallow, through my nose or mouth or maybe both at the same time." He moved his head an inch to the left, thought about it and moved it back a half an inch, decided to clench his fists and place them next to his thighs and opened his mouth into an enormous grin. "I think I'll take a nice slow deep breath."

As he murmured the words, he added speech to the things he could do and then quickly included singing, whistling, humming, plus all the emotional sounds, moaning, groaning, grunting, crying and the rest. With much the same deliberation that a connoisseur uses as he is about to enjoy a rare and costly brandy, the man prepared for his deep slow breath. He tested the air with several preliminary sniffs. He swallowed, then cleared his throat. Finally, he started sucking in the air slowly through his mouth until his lungs had expanded to their full capacity. Then equally slowly he allowed the air to escape from his nostrils. "That was good." He smacked his lips with satisfaction. "I must do that again real soon."

When finally the light of the coming morning began to find its way through the window curtains, the man wanted to shout out his delight. "It's growing lighter," he chortled, "soon there will be sunlight." The idea was delicious. "It will be light for hours and hours and people will come." He felt as if he owned a giant box filled with dozens of unopened presents. Doctors and nurses and attendants would be in and out of his room. He would be able to talk to each one. His bed would be changed and his back rubbed and so very many other things were about to start happening. And his wife would be coming to visit. This last was a treat so wonderful that the man found it hard to believe that it would actually happen. He allowed himself the pleasant torture of doubting. Somehow, this added a bit of delightful spice.

The sunlight finally filled the window, illuminating every part of the room. The man felt rich, more than he had ever known was possible. A whole day lay ahead. Nothing seemed important except that. When he wanted to, he could turn his mind for a moment onto his physical suffering, but each time his mind glanced off like a steel ball thrown against a rock.

Other, vastly more important things captured his attention.

"I am ready for my first visitor." The man said the words softly but took care to enunciate them carefully. "If anyone wants to enter my room, please feel free to do so." He turned his head toward the door and waited, wondering who it would be. Several minutes passed and the man continued to wait, confident that at any moment the door would open.

He smiled and nodded his head as the Negro orderly entered. "You expecting me?" the orderly asked with surprise. The man nodded his head. "You must be able to see through walls." The man continued to smile, but did not answer. "How you doing? I heard you tried to get out of bed last night."

"I did?" The man found it difficult to believe that it had happened so recently.

"That's what the male nurse told me. I just met him in the hall. You better be careful or you will slow down your recovery." The orderly shifted his body as if he were about to leave.

"Don't go," the sick man pleaded, "sit down for a little while and talk to me."

The orderly hesitated, then shrugged his shoulders. "I'm off duty," he started to explain. "But what the hell, I'll sit down and rest these weary bones for a few minutes."

"I sure appreciate your stopping by." The man reduced his voice to a whisper in order to conserve his energy. "It's nice to have company."

"That's OK." The orderly turned his head away in embarrassment. "I know it must get lonely, especially during the night. So, how you doing?"

The sick man carefully considered the question. Each word that came from the other man had great importance. Words were exciting and valuable. "I am doing all right. If I had a glass of water, things would be just about as good as I could ask."

The orderly jumped up and filled a glass from the sink, then lifted the patient's head and adjusted a flexible plastic straw between his lips. "Man, why didn't you call out and ask the nurse for some water? You act like you are dry clear down to the bone."

"I thought about it," the man allowed his head to fall back on the pillow, "but I had other things to do and I knew someone would be by sooner or later."

"You are all right!" the orderly smiled lovingly. "Other things to do," he repeated the sick man's words in a tone of wonder. "And you strapped down and weak as a kitten. Next thing I'll hear is you're all cured and on your way home."

"Didn't they tell you what's wrong with me?" The sick man sounded puzzled.

"Some kind of virus or something. That's what I heard. Some kind of infection."

"I have leukemia. I'll probably make it home for a while, but they doubt if I can last much longer than another six months. A year at the most. Didn't you know that?"

The orderly sagged in his seat. He started to speak, but instead licked his lips several times. Finally, after careful consideration, he answered in a voice several notes lower than usual. "Yes, I knew. I didn't think you knew. Don't hold it against me, man. I was just trying to cheer you up a little."

"Thank you." The sick man bowed his head until his chin touched his chest. "I understand."

"Ain't nobody in the hospital isn't pulling for you. Everyone wants to see you on your feet in time for the baby."

"Don't worry," the man winked one eye, "I'll make it all right."

"Sure you will. You look a hell of a lot better than yesterday," the orderly lied.

"I was pretty shook up when I first found out," the man whispered half to himself, "but I guess I've worked it out.

143

Everybody dies sometime, only in my case I know. In my case it isn't years away, just months. But a month is a long time. A day is a long time. You take each day by itself and don't worry about the next. I know I'm gonna last at least until the baby is born, and that is a big thing, a hell of a big thing. Why look any further?"

"I like the way you think, man." The orderly got up and went over to the bed. "You and me are plenty similar. I take it for each day. Baby, if I looked too far ahead and started to let it get me, I'd take the gas pipe or tear everything to pieces. We both got it plenty hard. Like you say, you figured it out, one day at a time. You keep thinking that way, hear!"

For several minutes after the orderly left the room the man kept mumbling, scarcely aware of what he was doing, "One day at a time, one day at a time."

# 31

The sick man lay partially naked on his bed watching the resident conduct the examination. Every time the doctor probed or manipulated a part of his body, he experienced a stab of pain. Some areas were far more sensitive than others. The man kept track of the less tender and more tender places and was able to calculate the degree of pain he might expect from an abdominal probe as compared to a chest tap. Even something as minor as pulling down the lower eyelid had its share of discomfort.

Despite the pain, which at times brought tears to his eyes, the man enjoyed the examination. He was sharply aware that it was his body that was being manipulated, yet he was able to be an interested observer in addition to being a subject. The examinations he had submitted to on preceding days ranged from distressing to actual torture. This time, although the pain was if anything more severe, he was glad for the attention and decided that his twice daily physical examinations were events he would look forward to. "As long as the pain is bearable, I won't let it bother me," he vowed after a particularly distressing probe up under his rib cage.

After the resident completed the physical examination he started to ask the patient various questions about how he felt.

The sick man answered several of the questions, then suddenly interrupted, "Doc, can I ask you something?" The resident grunted in the affirmative. The man smiled for a moment then in a quiet but earnest voice asked, "Why do you think I got this thing? I mean why me? Did I do something that brought it on?"

The resident looked at the patient, trying to determine if the man were serious. He felt himself growing annoyed but was not sure why. "I can assure you," the doctor forced himself to sound very precise, "that nothing you did or did not do made any difference. Leukemia is one of a number of diseases that medical science does not yet fully understand. Some people develop this condition; most do not. Someday we will know why."

"Doc," the man spoke coyly, "is it possible, what I mean, is there any chance that I don't have leukemia, that I have something that looks like it but isn't? Is it possible?"

The resident considered his answer carefully. He was tempted to answer yes, to allow the patient a tiny particle of hope. In the past he had not found it difficult to withhold from the man the truth about his condition, but when faced with a direct question about a diagnosis of which he was certain the resident found himself unable to prevaricate. "We are absolutely certain of the diagnosis," he said crisply. "I suggest that the best thing for you would be to put it out of your mind and concentrate on getting better so that we can send you home."

"All leukemia cases get better at first, don't they, doc?" The sick man still sounded coy although he was beginning to experience a tug of anxiety. All the good feelings he had carefully gathered were lessening, leaving behind a sick heaviness.

"I do not intend to discuss your medical problems with you any more today. I can see no point in this discussion. I will not assist you in working yourself into an anxiety state."

146

As he admonished his patient, the resident allowed his voice to rise so that it was noticeably louder than its usual professional level.

The resident got up and as he started to leave, the sick man called out as loud as he could, "Please can you take the straps off? I promise not to cause any trouble."

With a curt, "I'm sorry, no," the resident walked out of the room.

As he walked down the hall on the way to his next patient, the resident found himself growing increasingly angry. "He should never have been told his diagnosis," he muttered. "That old fool let the patient manipulate him into telling. Now all we can expect is endless questions, and when it comes down to it all any of us can answer is that we don't know. I wish to hell those old-timers with their damn bedside manners would leave my patients alone."

The resident reached the next patient's room. He was about to go in, but instead wheeled around and walked rapidly back to the nurse's station, giving the nurse orders to remove the restraining straps from the patient in 208.

# 32

The man lay absolutely still as the straps were being removed. He had lain immobile with his eyes tightly shut since the resident left the room, trying to recapture a portion of the peace he acquired during the early hours of the morning. He was cold and his flesh hung like sheets of crushing lead on his aching bones. He was grateful for the end of his confinement but afraid that if he opened his eyes or tried to thank the nurse, he would lose the little control he had left and start blubbering.

The room had grown smaller and the bare walls looked lifeless. Light filtering through the curtains seemed thick like dull grey paste. Everything felt decayed and very, very old.

The man slowly opened his eyes and groaned. The death-like quality of the room oozed through his eyeballs down into the hurting portion of his brain. Closing his eyes again, he tried to think of nothing, to be nothing. He allowed the pain to crawl over his body and drive away all other sensations. He became a mass of rotting pain, reddened flesh without thoughts or emotions. He didn't care if he lived or died. Nothing mattered; everything was grinding agony.

Suddenly he shuddered. He opened his eyes and shifted them wildly in every direction. The skin on the back of his neck tightened and pulled, and his face turned a damp cold.

"I am going to die." The words rasped in his throat. "There is nothing anyone can do to save me. I'm finished." The man balled his hands into fists, pressing them both over his open mouth. The rush of fear was so great it made him gasp. "Oh, no, please, no, it can't happen to me. Please, please, please." His throat was so tight and dry he was scarcely able to force the words out.

"What are you so upset about?" The man stopped gasping. A new thought that was almost like a voice inside his head forced him to listen. "You're acting like you're already dead. Calm down, take it easy." He pulled his white knuckled fists away from his mouth and allowed his hands to drop down on the bed. "They got you all shook up, like you're ready for the undertaker right now." His mouth closed and the tension started flowing out of his body. "How do you know you are going to die? Just because the doctors say so?"

The man rapidly shook his head from side to side. It was the only way he knew to stop the new flow of thoughts for enough time to allow him a chance to adjust himself. Without thinking about the pain, he found a more comfortable position in bed. Then he bunched the pillow up a little so that his head was lifted higher. Finally he placed his arms and legs so they would not have to be moved for a while, and closed his eyes.

"That disease you have is in you." The thought rang through the man's head and he silently repeated the words with his lips. The thoughts flooded out of his brain. "That disease inside of you is in your blood. It's your disease. Just like your heart and stomach belong to you, it belongs to you. All you have to do is figure out how to get that leukemia under control. No doctor can do it for you. They don't even understand exactly what it's all about. But you can control it yourself if you can only learn how."

"How?" The man whispered the one-word question.

"You can move each of your own muscles, can't you?" The man nodded in answer to his own question. "If you had to, if you really had to, if the hospital was burning down, you could get out of bed, couldn't you?" The man nodded again. "You do your own swallowing, you piss and shit. There's no doctor that does those things for you. All the doctors in this place together can't get inside your body and make it work. Everything you do is because of you."

The man felt the beginnings of the same bubbling sensation he had experienced the night before. But this time it seemed to be richer and more lasting.

"You can think about food; your mind thinks about food and you are hungry. Your mind brings up a picture of a naked girl and you get sexy. That mind of yours can do anything if you learn how to control it. You must use the force in your mind to stop this disease. The force is there, but only you can find it."

As if he were two people, the sick man answered his own thoughts: "Yes, yes, that's it. Only I can find it."

# 33

The woman got off the bus when it reached the bottom of the hill. She could have remained aboard and been carried to within a block of the hospital, but on an impulse decided to walk the last quarter of a mile. Disregarding her bulging abdomen she started up the hill, breathing the fresh chill air deep into her lungs, enjoying the cold sensation that developed in her throat and chest. It reminded her of the times she struggled up a snow-covered hill pulling her sled—the heavy breathing had hurt, but was part of the fun. Except for the weight of the baby, the woman still pulsed with the same glorious vitality of her childhood. The sky was so clean and blue after the wild storm of the night before. Her mouth tasted sweet; the flavor of mid-morning coffee and strawberry jam still lingered. The movements of her leg muscles and their pull on her buttocks and back as she marched up the hill were strangely satisfying.

All that morning the woman had been thinking about her husband. Her thoughts were not of the man who lay like an infant, helpless in his giant hospital crib. They were of the man she married and lived with. All morning she kept asking herself, "Did I love him? Did I really love him? Did he love me?" More bravely than ever before she had examined these

questions, trying out various answers and critically considering each one. By the time she was ready to leave home, she
had discarded the answers yes and no. "We felt about each
other much the same as most men and women who have been
married for a year and a half feel about each other," she
decided. "We got along, most of the time. It was good
enough. Not great, but good enough. He was an OK husband
and I was an OK wife. We were average, typical. Not a story-
book marriage; but whose is?"

She had enjoyed an extra cup of coffee to allow herself
sufficient time to determine her course of action for that day
and for as many days or months as her husband remained
alive. "He is my husband and he is sick and I am well. We
were married and I had no serious complaints. For as long as
he lasts, I will give him everything he needs to the limits of
my ability. I am not going to indulge in self-pity and I'm not
going to allow myself to get so upset that I am more of a
hindrance than a help."

As the woman walked up the hill, she reviewed her
thoughts and decisions. For the first time since her husband
had fallen sick, she was content with herself.

Standing before the main entrance to the hospital puffing
steam and slapping her arms against her body to keep warm,
was the fat woman. Her nose was an angry red and her eyes
were swollen and rheumy. The younger woman hesitated as
soon as she saw the other. For a moment she considered turning her head and pretending not to have seen her. Then,
strongly influenced by her mature thinking of the morning,
she smiled and said, "Hello."

"Mine is dying. How is yours?" The fat woman's voice
was very husky and it broke several times. Without waiting
for an answer she continued, turning her face away from the
younger woman, "I hate that son of a bitch for doing this."

The woman gasped. She felt as if the fat woman had punched her in the stomach.

"Don't tell me you don't feel that way too. I know better. Even with your cockeyed theory about how others, how we make them sick, I'll bet you're plenty sore at your old man."

"You should be ashamed of yourself," the young woman hissed. All her self-control was melting away like wax from a candle thrown into a furnace. "You are a vile and disgusting person." She tightened her fists and wanted to smash the other's bloated face.

"See, I knew it. I knew it," the fat woman cackled. "If I wasn't right, you wouldn't be mad. You are just like me. I hate mine for dying. He is going to be dead and that's the end of it for him. But I'll be left. He is leaving me, the son of a bitch. I'm not leaving. I didn't make myself sick so I have to die. That's why you have that phony theory of yours. If you think it was your fault, yours and all the bad thoughts of all the bad, bad people, then you can't let yourself feel mad at him. I've been married to my old man for more than thirty years and he is about to go away forever and there is not a damn thing I can do."

The young woman was shocked by the fat woman's torrent of words. She wanted to turn around and run into the hospital; she wanted to cover her ears and shout, "No! No!" More than anything she wanted to hit the woman, but instead she did not move.

"The doctors say that mine won't last another day. You should see him; he looks like a sawdust doll without the sawdust. They have tubes going in and out of him. What a disgusting mess. I hate to look at him."

"You should be ashamed," the young woman whispered mechanically.

"I married a great big strapping handsome fellow. Women

used to turn around on the street to look at him, and now he's just a bluish bag of skin. That bastard has taken everything away—his looks, his youth, and now he is going to take away his life. I hate him."

The young woman looked at the fat woman's face. It had been turned partially away, but one of her eyes was visible. "You've been crying!" Wonder filled the young woman's voice. "If you hate him so much, why have you been crying?"

The fat woman turned her face. Tears filled both eyes; some had spilled out and wet her cheeks. "Don't you understand anything?" she whispered. "My heart is breaking, that's why I'm crying. My husband of thirty years is dying. Don't you understand?"

# 34

The woman remained standing in front of the hospital for
several minutes after the fat woman left. She might have remained there for hours if the weather had not been so cold.
She did not want to leave the sky and the air. She thought
vaguely of going to her husband and carrying him outdoors in
her arms, placing him on the earth and showing him the sky.
She wondered how anyone could get well inside that stone
and steel structure. She wished she could turn around and go
away from the hospital and never come back .

The man appeared to be sleeping when his wife entered
the room, but his eyes opened as soon as he heard her footsteps. "I sure am glad to see you." His voice rasped as he
made an effort to speak normally. "I've been hoping you
would come. I sure am glad to see you," he repeated.

"You needn't worry about me not visiting. I intend to be
here every day, rain or shine."

"How is it outside?" As if the man had known her
thoughts he blurted out, "I'd give an awful lot to be outside
right now. Too bad you can't just pick me up and carry me
down to the street. It would be good to look up at the sky."

"How did you know?" The woman took a step backward,
then eased over to the other side of the room and sat down.

The man looked puzzled, but didn't answer. She started giggling nervously. "You are a regular mind reader. You must have learned it since you came here."

"I don't understand." The man raised his eyebrows a little. "You aren't making sense."

"Just before, as I was about to come into the hospital, I thought about how nice it would be if you could lie on the ground and breathe fresh air for a while. Just like you said, I thought about carrying you down myself (as if I could), and then as soon as I came into the room you said the same thing."

The man considered his wife's words, then changed the subject. "Have you talked to anyone yet?" he asked sheepishly, "the resident or the nurse?" The woman shook her head. "I am on the shit list." He grinned and turned his eyes toward the ceiling. "Last night for a little while I was feeling pretty good. Well anyhow, to make a long story short, I tried to get out of bed." He grinned more openly. "I decided to come home and keep you company." He stopped and waited uneasily for his wife's reaction.

"I understand." She spoke as if she were in a dream state. "If I had to lie in that bed day after day, I probably would do the same thing."

The man had expected his wife to admonish him, to warn him to be careful, and he was surprised at her reaction. "They strapped me down until a couple of hours ago. Probably will again tonight."

"I'll speak to the doctor." The woman's words were uttered half as a statement, half as a question.

"Tell him that I won't try to get out of bed tonight. Tell him I've learned my lesson."

"I'll tell him." The woman wrinkled her forehead, then patted her hair, her fingers searching for stray strands. "You sound different," she said slowly. "You sound like you know something, like you do when you bring home a present and don't want me to know."

"I haven't been lying here all this time just wasting my time." The man spoke cautiously. The white gauze mask made it difficult to gauge his wife's reaction.

"Wasting your time?"

"I've been thinking. Thinking harder than I ever did before. You know something?" The man propped his head up several inches, using his upper arm as a pillow. "Before I came here I scarcely ever took time out to think. I doubt if I spent five minutes a week just thinking."

"You think all the time," his wife interrupted. "Even when you are asleep, they say the mind still is working."

"That's not what I mean," the man explained patiently. "I'm not talking about whether your brain is working all the time. I mean coming up with original thoughts, with something new, like Robinson Crusoe having to figure things out on that desert island."

The woman nodded her understanding and started to comment but her husband cut her off. "Let me finish. Let me explain while it's all clear in my mind. You know that the doctors don't understand very much about leukemia. I'm beginning to believe there are lots of things they don't know much about. They know what happens to you when you get leukemia; you die. But they don't know why you get it or how to cure it. All they can do is keep you going for a while, sometimes. OK. Everybody knows that you can make yourself sick by worrying and that even cripples can force themselves to walk again. You read about people with the will to live coming through terrible diseases, about patients with bad hearts or lungs outliving their doctors. You hear about these things all the time—even with dying cancer patients, like we talked about, one in ten thousand suddenly gets well."

157

The man stopped speaking; he was short of breath and at the same time wanted to give his wife an opportunity to assimilate his words. She remained silent, but showed with her eyes that she was listening carefully.

"I've done it myself," the man continued. "I've talked myself into feeling lousy. I remember going out with a girl who came down with strep throat the next day; I had pains in my throat for a week. And there were times I had something important to do and didn't feel too well and was able to snap myself out of being sick. OK. So you see that the mind, the human mind, is a powerful thing. Look at all the things human beings have invented. I have this disease. Someday the power of the human mind will find a cure for this disease like they can cure pneumonia right now. So you have the power of the human mind. You know that people can make themselves sick or well, and you have this disease inside of you. If I can learn how to concentrate all the power of my mind, if I can learn the trick of using every atom of my brain, I am convinced I can cure this sickness."

"But all the doctors and scientists working to find a cure . . ." the woman stopped speaking without finishing the sentence.

"I thought about that." The man's eyes burned with excitement. "I am not trying to invent a drug or something like that. When they have a drug or treatment, everyone who has leukemia will be cured. I am only working on myself, on my own personal disease. A thousand doctors, ten thousand doctors all concentrating their brains on my condition are not equal to the power in me. If every doctor in the whole world were here in this room, all their knowledge together couldn't make me swallow or say something or not say something. Only I can. You see what I mean? With all their smartness, they can't get inside my nerves, into my bones and veins; but I can, because I am inside me."

The man looked into his wife's eyes and held them for several seconds. They were opened wider than normal, the pupils riveted on his. "Do you see what I am getting at?" he asked. "I have to learn how to use the full strength of my brain to root out this damn rotten disease and destroy it." The man paused and tried to catch his breath; his lips were wet with spittle and there were patches of blotchy red on his cheeks. "If I can learn how to use the force inside my mind," he panted, "once I learn how I am certain I can get well."

Her husband's words scorched the woman's ears. Several times she had had the impulse to yell out, "Stop fighting, stop burning up the little energy you have left." She wanted to plead with him to take it easy and concentrate on getting better so that he would be able to come home for a while. His eyes and his labored breathing frightened her. She listened to his words, but only a portion of them found their way inside. When he had finished speaking she did not know what to say. "He has it all worked out," she thought, "poor thing. He has convinced himself."

After remaining silent for more than a minute, realizing that she was expected to say something, the woman started speaking. She selected each word carefully and spoke slowly. "You certainly have been thinking. I'm not sure I understand everything you said. I agree the human mind is very powerful. I can't argue about that." The woman paused. She thought about the decisions she had reached that morning. "If he wants to believe he can make himself well," she decided, "what harm is there in it?" Her exchanges with the fat woman crossed her mind. "If negative thoughts can make you sick, why not the reverse?" A tiny wedge was opened into her mind. "You never know about these things. Suppose there is one chance in a million . . ." She cleared her throat. "Did you consider," she felt dishonest sounding so serious when she had so many reservations, "did you give any thought to the

159

possibility that others, other people's minds working together with yours might produce more strength? They say that it is not only what you do to yourself, but also what others do to you."

"No, I never thought about that," the man murmured, "like people praying together for something." He chewed on his lower lip for several seconds. "That makes sense." He spoke so softly his words were scarcely audible. "It is my mind that has to actually do the job, but other people using the force of their brains . . . maybe that's why so few succeed. You need more than your own strength."

"You look so tired," the woman spoke tenderly. "If you like, I'll sit here while you sleep for a little while."

The man brushed his wife's words away with a feeble wave of his hand. "I'll sleep when I'm ready." He did not try to conceal his irritation. "I'm no infant that needs to be constantly told what to do."

"I'm sorry," the woman sighed. "I was only trying to follow the doctor's orders not to overtire you."

"I didn't mean to snap at you. I'll rest in a little while. I am tired, but I want to get everything in order in my head before I go to sleep." The man frowned and held the frown while he considered what had been discussed. After a long pause, he again shared his thinking with his wife. "It's like going to war, only the battlefield is inside my body. I have to fight a battle with the enemy and destroy it. This damn disease is my enemy—it is trying to kill me. The more I think about it, the more sense your idea makes. To fight a battle you need all the ammunition you can get. I supply the troops, in a manner of speaking, and you together with as many others as possible provide the ammunition. Some of the ammunition will come from me, but I'll need help, no doubt about it." The man's eyes filled with the same feverish frantic look they'd had earlier. "I haven't figured it all out yet, but

I'm getting closer. I need a little more time. As soon as I am ready, I'll need your help. Your help most of all, but I'll have to have others also. By tomorrow I should have her all worked out."

The woman fidgeted in her chair. Her husband's words had grown meaningless to her. She forced herself to listen because he was sick and wanted to talk, but her mind had drifted off. At one point she found herself beginning to believe that there might be a chance, however slight, but that point had passed. Now she was just waiting for him to finish.

"I can count on you helping me, can't I?" The man's eyes began closing. He was so exhausted he found it difficult to form his words. "Can't I?" he whispered as his lids fluttered shut.

"Of course, you can count on me. Next time I come to see you, we'll talk about it some more. I'll be back tomorrow. I don't want to tire you any more today." The woman felt a little guilty about not returning that afternoon; had the man so much as hinted that he wanted her back, she would have changed her plans. She waited for his reaction. After several minutes, realizing he was asleep, she tiptoed out of the room. "It will be better for him if I don't come back this afternoon," she told herself. "He gets himself so excited . . . I'm glad he has something to hold onto . . . it can't hurt to agree with him. I'll do anything he wants, anything to keep him happy, poor sick baby."

# 35

The room had grown very large and was filled with red and yellow flowers, thousands of flowers. From these flowers rose an odor so rich it made the man deliciously dizzy. The room was open to the sky and except for a thin curl of translucent cloud, the sky was a roof of shimmering crystal. The man's wife sat next to his bed; her gauze mask could not hide her smile. The man's body was light; every movement of his arms and legs flowed effortlessly out of the center of his being.

His wife smiled and smiled; several times she nodded and touched her belly. "Put your hand out," she whispered, "come on, come on, it's your baby." The man wanted to touch his wife, but was shy. Everything was so beautiful he blushed with embarrassment. "Touch your baby, touch your baby," she breathed. He leaned over and placed his palm on her abdomen. Inside he could feel wonderful things, moving, growing, pulsing things. His hand tingled.

He looked up and was bathed in the glow of his wife's happy face. "In a little while you will be able to hold the baby in your arms," she crooned. "Just wait a little longer, try and wait a little longer."

"May I listen to the baby?" he asked in a tiny voice. "I promise to be careful." The woman gently nodded her head.

He placed his ear against her body, then pressed in tight. She cradled his head with her arm as he listened.

It sounded like water when you swim down toward the bottom. It sounded like a tree trembling in the wind. It sounded like a great waterfall a mile away.

The man felt himself slowly sinking into his wife's body. He moved into the dark of her being, into a warmth so perfect that no pain or hunger could ever reach him. He lay in the rich fluid, letting it bathe and mingle with his substance. He reached out and clasped his sleeping baby to his bosom and rocked the infant, taking care not to disturb its sleeping.

A minute or a year passed. The man felt himself being pulled by the arm out of the warmth. He tried to struggle but was helpless. He squeezed his eyelids tightly shut to hold the darkness, but the cold light seeped through the tissue into his brain.

He opened his eyes and stared up into the face of the resident. "Why did you do that to me?" he groaned. "Why didn't you let me stay?"

The resident shone the beam of his pencil flashlight into each of the patient's eyes. "I'll be through in a few minutes and you can go back to sleep," he mumbled. "Sorry I had to wake you up."

The man looked around the room. It was small—all the flowers had disappeared. "Where are all the flowers, and where is the sky?" He wanted to cry, the room had grown so close and ugly. "Where is my wife?"

"She went home. You've been asleep for hours. Did someone send you flowers?" The resident continued his examination as he spoke.

"The room was filled with flowers. They were everywhere."

"You must have been dreaming."

"Dreaming? I must have been dreaming? Yes, I guess so," the man sighed. "You should have seen them, they looked so beautiful. Too bad they weren't real." He sighed again.

"Are you having any pain?" The resident started writing in the patient's chart.

"Am I having any pain?" The man carefully considered the question. He hadn't thought about pain in quite a while. "I guess so. I haven't paid much attention to it, but I guess it's there."

"You guess it's there." The resident looked over the top of the chart with an irritated expression on his face. "Are you having any pain, yes or no, and if so, where and how much?"

"You sound like a lawyer," the man tittered, "guilty or not guilty, your honor."

The resident lowered the chart and frowned at the patient; the corners of his mouth were tightened with annoyance.

"No offense intended." The man tried to control his voice so that he sounded serious. "I do have some pain. Not as bad as before, but it's there. I've been thinking about other things so I haven't paid much attention to how I feel."

"Any unusual shortness of breath or other unusual symptoms?"

"No. Everything is about the same. I'm tired of lying here in this bed, that's all."

"Bed rest is essential. We want to conserve every bit of your energy possible."

"My energy is important, isn't it?" the man asked, seeking additional information from the doctor.

"Essential. Your progress depends largely on your body's ability to fight off infection and its capacity to stabilize the condition."

"Would you say," the man tried to sound casual, "that the desire to get better plays an important part in a patient's chances of getting better?"

The resident's eyes narrowed. "Do you mean does your attitude affect your chances of improving?"

164

"Yes. Can my thinking help me?"

"The desire to get better is absolutely essential. Without that, even the best doctors using the most modern techniques are seriously handicapped."

"I thought so. The mind is a very powerful thing, isn't it? The power of the human mind is so great, we scarcely know anything about it. Isn't that true?"

"As much as I might like to engage in a theoretical discussion with you, I am afraid I cannot." The resident made a final entry in the chart. "The workings of the mind are the least understood function of the body. It's as little known as the bottom of the ocean."

"Do you have another minute?" The man caught the resident's eyes and held them.

"Well, if it won't wait, go ahead."

"I have been thinking—very carefully. What you just said only makes me more certain. I've been able to figure out certain things. I know how I can get well." The man paused, waiting for a reaction from the other, but the resident did not alter his expression. "If I can concentrate all the powers of my mind on this leukemia inside of me—I'll need help, but the major task I have to do myself—if I can use every atom of force in my mind, I can beat this disease."

The resident's expression remained unchanged. "You said a minute and the minute is up. You concentrate on getting better and sleep as much as possible." Without giving the man a chance to say another word, the resident walked out of the room.

"He didn't believe me." The man shrugged his shoulders as he thought about the doctor's abrupt departure. "I wasn't able to explain it right. I'll think about it some more and by tomorrow I'll have it down pat. He did agree that the human mind is a powerful thing." The man began to whisper to himself. "He said that the desire to get well is absolutely essential . . . that only confirms my thinking." He started grinning, then chuckled. "You thought you could kill me, didn't you!" He placed both hands on his stomach and dug his fingers into the skin, unconcerned with the sharp pains that were produced. "You son of a bitch, you are in for a great big surprise. You think you're incurable; well, I've got news for you —this time you lose." He began to laugh. "This is one kid you are not going to kill, do you understand?" The man's voice rose in pitch. "You lousy stinking sneaky bastard, you crawl inside and hide in the bones. You don't fight fair—do you hear me? I'm calling you a coward!" The man began to shout. "This time, you son of a bitch, you lose. This time you're up against someone who knows how to kill you!"

The man screamed out his hate. The sound was an unintelligible mixture of curses and threats. His hands clawed at his stomach, digging deeper and deeper into the skin. When the nurse rushed into his room, he found the patient rolling from side to side, his mouth and chin covered with foam. He bared the patient's arm to administer a hypodermic and saw that the man's fingers were stained with blood from the dozens of deep scratches on his abdomen.

"Why do you think he scratched himself?" the nurse asked the resident after they finished working on the patient.

"The pain may have suddenly become unbearable. We better use an increased dosage of sedation. . . . and just before I left his room, he was talking about getting well." The corners of the resident's mouth twitched as he spoke. "He seemed to have himself under control, then twenty minutes later . . . He will have to be restrained. Could you make any sense out of what he was screaming?"

"Sounded like a bunch of gibberish, a few curse words and the rest gibberish. He didn't know what he was saying."

# 36

"How do you feel, young fellow?" The man opened his narcotic-dulled eyes. "They tell me you were a little upset before. Is something the matter?" The man tried to sharpen the outlines of the waving blurred image. "Is there anything I can do for you?" The man opened his mouth as if to speak, then closed it as he struggled to identify the form hovering over him. "That's all right; if you are too tired, you don't have to answer."

"It's old slime cola," the sick man mumbled.

"That's right, you hit it right on the button."

"I'm getting better." The man's speech was slurred, making it difficult to understand.

"Of course you are. You get plenty of sleep and don't worry about anything. No more wild scenes, do you understand, young man?"

"Figured out how to get well. Still working on it. Tell you about it later."

"That's nice. Now go to sleep. I'll be back in the morning."

"No kidding, doc. You don't have to worry, I ain't gonna die."

"Shissh, close your eyes and go to sleep; doctor's orders."

"Slime cola," the sick man weakly chuckled, "that's a funny name for a doctor . . ."

The wind whipped sharp bits of snow and ice in every direction. Everybody hunched against the wind, covering their faces with their arms. Despite the furious gusts, there was no sound. The people moved up and down the street without speaking. It was a cruel cold; needles of ice formed in people's nostrils. All were shivering.

The man walked down the street wearing his hospital gown. He was barefoot and bareheaded and he walked erect. The icy air felt like silk against his skin. All the bluish frozen people struggling against the cold surprised him. They were wrapped in coats and scarves, encased in thick shoes and gloves, yet they hunched like toads. The cold was delicious. Why was everybody afraid to enjoy it? Why were they trembling and hiding their faces?

"They are all sick, poor people," the man told himself. "Some terrible epidemic must have swept through the city. They are all suffering so; they need help so they can get well again."

The man stopped and looked in every direction. All around him were grey sick people covered with frost, moving aimlessly, silently. He was the only one who had escaped the disease. The rest had been struck by a plague that caused the marrow of their bones to turn to ice.

"If I don't help them," the man thought, "everyone will die. How fortunate that I should come along at this time."

He reached out and tried to stop one of the passersby, but the other shrank back, eluding his touch. He reached out again and was scarcely able to get the tips of his fingers on the slinking person before he scurried away. They all looked the same, grey and feeble, moving slowly except when he tried to touch them. Then they hurried.

168

"Listen, all of you sick people," he shouted at the top of his voice, "I have a marvelous thing to tell you." The grey beings kept moving; none stopped. None listened. "I had what you now have and look—," he lifted the upper part of the gown, "see how healthy I am. See my glowing skin, see how the cold does not burn me." Nobody stopped and nobody listened. "You have the power within yourselves," he shrieked into the silent muffling air. "If you will only fight the frost—the heat of your minds will warm your bones. Look at me, look at me." He pulled off the top of his gown and threw it away. "All the snow and sleet, and I feel nothing." He opened his arms wide and brought them toward his body as if to gather armfuls of frigid air.

"They won't listen to me," he groaned. As the words passed out of his mouth, his lips were chilled. "Please stop and listen and believe me." The chill spread upward to his nose and eyes and down over his chin into his neck. The man felt himself beginning to freeze. "If only one of you will stop and hear my words, I can save you." He trembled with fear and cold. "If no one stops and believes, I will become like you," he moaned, "and if I do, I will die." He wrapped his arms tightly about his bluish body. "I have no clothing and will die now, while you may live for a little time."

The man, with the sudden movement of a panther, grabbed one by the arm and saw the person's face. "Doctor," he cried, "listen to me. I know how to cure all diseases." The resident shrank away, hiding his face again without a sound, without a flicker of recognition. The cold was stiffening the man's body. Desperately he reached for another person and uncovered the face of the nurse. He hesitated for a moment then pulled back. The shadowy people all around were suddenly familiar. The man recognized them all. "Don't you know who I am?" he gasped. "Isn't there one who will stop and believe me?" He clutched his wife, holding her with

169

every atom of energy he had left. "Don't you want to live?" The ice forming in his throat choked him. The words were scarcely audible. The woman tenderly pushed him away, shaking her head gently. Soundlessly she formed the words, "poor baby," then moved among the wandering people.

The man sank down and stretched out on the pavement, prepared to die. The people moved round and round him, their faces showing tenderness, their eyes wet with tears. All their lips were forming words of comfort. Some bent down and touched his stiffening body; but none shared their coat with the freezing man, and none listened and believed.

Every inch of his body throbbed and ached as the man struggled out of his sleep. His skin burned as if it were exposed to a blazing bonfire. Yet his insides, especially his bones, were cold, colder than he had ever known. He remembered standing before a great bonfire and pulling away from its searing heat while his back ached from the cold. He remembered turning around and warming his back while the rest of him cooled. By turning and turning he found he could enjoy both the cold and the fire. "If I turned round and round," he wondered, "could I mix the cold of the inside with the heat on my skin?" He tried to turn over but was held fast by the straps that crossed the bed. He thought of calling for the nurse, but the effort of filling his lungs and forming the words was more than he could muster.

He still could see himself lying on the sidewalk with the crowd of silent people gathered round. The dream hovered like a pall of choking vapor in the room and kept threatening to return and overwhelm him.

"I know how to get well." Mechanically and with great effort he whispered the words loud enough so that he could hear them. "Just a little more thinking and I'll have it all down pat." The cold inside him and the silent waiting people made him cry, but he tried not to pay attention to his crying. "I'm lucky I found out in time," he continued to whisper between sobs. "Would have been a tough break for me if I had died first."

He tried to reconstruct the details of his reasoning that earlier had seemed so clear, but the thoughts would not come. He knew he had worked out the logic; and he tried to force his brain to function properly, but all it could do was repeat the formula that had grown magical: "I know how to get well."

"Suppose I had not learned in time?" He fought the panic that began to flicker around the edges of his brain. "Suppose I had been unlucky like the rest." He tensed as the panic threatened to engulf him. "Suppose you died?" Another part of his mind started working and the panic evaporated as he considered the proposition. "You can't live forever. Suppose you die today or tomorrow or next month instead of say in fifty years, so what?"

"In fifty years I will have lived my life," he answered himself. "I will be ready to die."

"The hell you will! If you were fifty years older right now, you would be struggling just as hard to stay alive."

"Just give me the chance and I'll show you. If I can live another fifty years," the sick man tried to lift his arm to make a pledge, but the straps held it fast. He flexed his hand a little, counting that gesture as an adequate substitution. "If I can live another fifty years," he listened to the sound of 'fifty years' and repeated it, "fifty years, I swear I will not fight death. I'll be glad to die."

"Why will things be different in fifty years?"

"Because," the man chose each word carefully, "in fifty years I will be finished, all my tasks will be done. If I die now, in a little while it will be as if I had never lived. Nothing will be left."

171

"And in fifty years?"

"If I live another fifty years," the man flexed his hand again lifting it as far as it would go, "I solemnly swear my life will have an effect."

"An effect?"

"Yes, on others. My living will have made a difference."

"How will it have made a difference?" the other part of his mind taunted.

"I will have had a chance to do important things, to make a contribution to humanity."

"What important things, what sort of contribution?"

The man struggled to answer himself. So much of his thinking was confused. He clenched his jaws until little rockets of pain shot through his skull. Perspiration broke out on his forehead and his insides started moving in a horribly familiar fashion. "I don't know," he sobbed. "I don't know!" His body shook with the spasms of crying. "I can't think. My mind won't work."

"Fifty years," he jeered at himself, "fifty or a hundred years. It will make no difference. When you are gone, you will be forgotten and it will be as if you never lived."

"Please, God, let me live," the man whimpered. "I will try and be important. I will try with all my heart to deserve to live."

Suddenly—as if washed by a fresh wind—his mind cleared. Why torture himself any longer with waiting and wondering? Take a chance! He carefully composed his features and shut his eyes tight. "I might as well find out right now. If I have to die, why wait and suffer? I'll know in a minute." His thoughts turned to whispers. "If I am going to die, I am ready to die as soon as I say 'now.' Then if I do not die, it's proof that I can live and get well." He gasped several times, filling his lungs with air. "If I do not die, it will be proof that I can get well, that the strength of my mind can cure me." He tensed his body, clenching his fists and curling his toes. "When I say 'now' either I will die or I will know that I can live." The man pressed his eyelids down so tight that colors started whirling around in his brain. He took one final gulp of air and gasped out, "NOW!"

Icy drops of perspiration dripped from his skin as he waited. The colors danced and spun behind his lids. He held his breath, feeling his heart batter against his ribs. "Now!" He forced the little breath he had left to utter the word for the second time. His lungs were starved for air; a roaring sounded in his ears. He tried to take a breath, but his throat would not open. Then with a desperate gasp, he filled his lungs. His heart pounded so rapidly that it felt like one continuous shudder. Perspiration covered his body, soaking the bed clothes, collecting in every crevice, in every fold of skin.

"Now," he murmured for the third time, but he already knew he had won and was just offering the courtesy of a final chance.

He smiled. "Well, you made it," he said softly. "Nothing more for you to worry about." He started giggling. "For a second there I thought it was all over. Wow! When I couldn't get my breath . . ." The man's body softened as every muscle relaxed. He felt as if he were lying in a tub of warm water. "Sometimes you have to take a chance," he mumbled. "In order to know, you have to take a chance sometimes." He sighed and giggled again; then still smiling, he sank into a deep dreamless sleep.

# 37

The resident entered the room several hours before his regular tour of duty was scheduled to begin. The sun had not yet risen and the room was dark. The doctor, unshaven and peevish, peered at the sleeping man. He was irritated at himself for not being able to leave concern for his patients behind when he went off duty. "You act like a mother hen with her brood of chicks," he muttered. "If you expect to live to a ripe old age, you better learn how to relax, doctor." He leaned over the patient's bed, listening carefully to the sleeping man's breathing. "Better listen to his lungs," he decided and started fumbling for his stethoscope, then stopped. "Let him sleep a little longer." He pushed the stethoscope back into his pocket. "Why the hell you had to drag your ass out of bed this early, I don't know." The resident took a step backwards, then changed his mind again. "You were so damned worried about your patient that you couldn't sleep—now that you're here, you might as well satisfy yourself or you won't be able to sleep again."

The sick man opened his eyes as he felt the chill of the stethoscope on his chest. He lay still, watching the doctor work, trying unsuccessfully to see the resident's facial expression. The room was too dark. When the doctor removed the stethoscope from his ears, the man whispered, "Good morning." He wanted to speak in a normal voice, but all he could manage was the whisper. "I feel better; weak as a kitten, but better."

"You were pretty upset last night." The resident started probing the patient's armpits as he spoke. "You sound better today."

"I am better. You don't have to worry about me, doc. I'm gonna make it."

The resident got up and switched on the light. He turned to the man, whose face radiated contentment. "You look like you slept well—do you have any discomfort?"

"I ache." The man smiled, crinkling the corners of his eyes. "I never knew there was so much of me to ache, but I'm getting better. I can feel it."

"Very good, I am very pleased." The resident checked the patient's eyes, then looked into his nose and ears. "If you feel better, that is so much to the good, but it is no sign that we can stop taking precautions. I don't want you to let yourself get excited or to move more than is absolutely necessary. Sleep, sleep and more sleep, as little talking as possible—understand?"

"I'll bet that my insides sound better." The man winked at the doctor. "I'll take it easy, weak as I am; all I want to do is sleep. But the worst is over and I'm going to get well. I told you I was working on using all the power of my mind—last night I proved that it works. My insides do sound better, don't they?"

The resident stood up and without answering the man's question stated, "My best advice to you is to stop thinking about yourself and sleep. We want to get you on your feet, hopefully before your wife gives birth. But if you keep working yourself into a distressed state like you did last night, we may not be successful. You are in good hands; let us do the worrying."

175

The patient nodded his head. "I'm not going to worry. And doc," he winked his eye again, "don't you worry either. I really am going to get well."

Instead of finishing his interrupted sleep, the resident went down to the staff dining room. He was grumpy, irritable and dissatisfied and hoped some hot coffee would make him feel better. The intern who had worked with him on this patient was sitting at one of the tables and waved him over.

"Have an emergency?" the intern asked as the other sat down. "I thought only us lowly interns were up at this hour."

"I wanted to check on a patient; he was acting peculiar last night, and I thought I better look in on him to make sure."

"Anything interesting?"

"You know the patient. The young fellow with leukemia."

The intern nodded. "I meant to drop over and take a look at him, but I've been rushed. How is he doing?"

"He looked a little better this morning. The physical examination showed essentially the same signs as yesterday, but the patient reported feeling better and he seemed less agitated."

"What happened to him last night?" the intern asked.

With a weary sigh the resident picked up his coffee cup and took a long sip, closing his eyes as the warm liquid flowed into his mouth. "He has a theory," the resident removed the cup from his mouth for a moment, "that he can cure himself of leukemia."

"Then he knows." The intern raised his eyebrows. "I thought you weren't going to tell him."

"It was that ass of a family doctor." The resident banged his coffee cup on the table, spilling the few remaining drops. "He had to open his big mouth and now instead of sleeping and having his mind free of worry, the patient is burning up his energy trying to develop some magical way to cure his disease."

"Poor kid," the intern murmured.

"Last night he got so upset, he scratched his abdomen. When I first examined him I thought it was a reaction to a sudden episode of pain, but now I'm almost sure he was, in his own mixed-up way, trying to fight the disease. He is convinced that by the use of mind power he can cure himself. Just a minute ago, after I finished examining him, he told me not to worry." The resident uttered a nervous laugh. "He winked his eye and told me not to worry, that he was going to get well."

"Are you worried?" the intern asked with a chuckle.

"If I weren't concerned about my patients, I wouldn't be much of a doctor. I'm giving the kid everything, packed red blood cells, the latest word in chemotherapy, everything. With a little luck I'll have him back on his feet; he might go six or more months without a recurrence—give him a chance to be around when his baby comes and for a while after. But if he expends all his strength trying to harness some mystical mind force, he won't make it. When I left him, he was smiling like a medical student with a brand new degree. With an attitude of 'I know it all' he won't cooperate and he'll burn himself out. You know how it is with these acute cases, they pick up an infection like that—," the resident snapped his fingers, "and then you're fighting to keep them alive."

"I don't know," the intern rubbed his mouth with the palm of his hand, "sounds to me as if you're emphasizing the loss of energy and what may possibly happen, but not taking into consideration the effect upon the patient of his heightened morale."

The resident turned a deep scarlet. His lack of sleep and irritated state made him unusually short-tempered. "It sounds to you as if I am not taking into consideration my patient's morale. Don't you think you are being a bit presumptuous, doctor?" Without waiting for the other to reply, the resident continued, speaking in an exceedingly precise school-teacher-ish manner, "Impertinent might be a better word. I can assure you, doctor, that I am just as aware of morale factors as you are."

"Look," the intern suddenly felt his own temper rising, "I don't think there is any need for one doctor to call another impertinent. I made an observation, a medical observation. If you already considered the question of morale, then my observation was not useful to you, that's all."

"Forget it." The resident, although still angry, was unable to see how he could continue the argument with any profit. He was about to get up and had already pushed his chair away from the table, but instead turned to his younger colleague with a smirk on his face. "Since you are so interested in matters relating to morale, you might find it worth your while to evaluate the merits of my patient's theory regarding the management and cure of leukemia and other like maladies. If the theory meets with your learned medical approval, we might then conduct courses amongst our terminal patients on the proper use of mind power. Perhaps my patient can even become a member of the hospital staff and teach the course—with your expert assistance, naturally, doctor."

"Naturally." The intern reacted to the other's ridicule as if it were a serious suggestion. He was very angry, but kept his feelings well hidden. "I appreciate your suggestion and the first chance I get, this afternoon at the latest, I will drop over and see your patient and listen to his theory. Frankly, it sounds most interesting. We doctors have our theories about leukemia, but none of ours include a method for its cure. It strikes me that any theory that suggests a cure is at least worth considering. Not that I am suggesting that doctors as a general rule can learn from their patients, perish forbid!"

"You do that." The resident tightened his lips into a thin

bluish smile. "You visit the patient—he is in Room 208. Medical history is about to be made!"

The intern narrowed his eyes and leaned a few inches toward the other doctor. "I'll tell you something in confidence. Don't repeat it to more than a hundred people. Even before I have a chance to speak to him, I think that patient of yours has a theory worth considerable thought. Wouldn't everybody be surprised if he pulled it off? I'm looking forward to our conference."

"If you write a paper, doctor," the resident arose from the table as he spoke, "which name will appear first, yours or the patient's?"

"The patient's, of course. Since he is your patient, it would be only fitting if your name were included also."

The resident snorted, and walked rapidly away.

"That last one really burned his ass," the intern chuckled. "He'll probably find an excuse to give me a lousy write-up . . . The hell with it," he muttered. "I'm tired of crawling on my belly. Patients are not people to him. They are bodies to be treated and kept alive, and when nothing works and the bodies die, they are subjects for post-mortem examinations; then on to the next patient."

The intern drummed on the table with his fingers. "He thought I was fooling. Well, maybe I was at first," he decided, "but the only way to stop him from throwing his weight around is to call his bluff. I'll go up after lunch and listen to the poor kid's cockeyed theory. There's no harm in humoring him. I swear, I'd argue that the moon is made out of green cheese just to show that cold fish that he isn't so superior."

179

# 38

Just before the regular morning visiting hour the ambulance attendant, still dressed in street clothes, tapped on the sick man's door. Without waiting for permission he stuck his head in. "Remember me?" he grinned, "I'm the one who rode with you in the ambulance. Just thought I'd drop by and see how you're doing."

The man nodded at his visitor but was unable to recall his face. "Thanks for thinking about me; I guess I was pretty sick when you brought me in. Sit down and rest yourself."

"You're in reverse isolation; I can't come in without taking the proper precautions. Just wanted to say hello. How're you doing?" The ambulance attendant was still grinning; he appeared to be excited about something.

"I'm better, thanks. Awfully nice of you to think of me."

"I promised your wife I'd look in on you. She's a brave little soldier."

"Best there is," the man answered quietly.

"You hurry up and get well. You don't want to leave a woman like that alone too long. A woman like that needs the protection of a man."

"With her belly as big as it is," the man chuckled, "I suspect she is safe for at least the next couple of months."

"You never know," the ambulance attendant said, "plenty of weirdos floating around. If she was my wife, I would want to be available as much as possible. So you make it your business to get well."

"Don't worry about me. I'll be out of this place soon." A trace of annoyance altered the man's voice. "And I appreciate your concern about my wife; but as long as I am around, you don't have to trouble your mind much about her."

"Of course; just wanted to let you know that you have friends here in the hospital who are concerned and are rooting for you." The ambulance attendant put the tip of his forefinger on the tip of his thumb, making a circle. "You're all right. Lots of fight still left in you. I'm betting on you to make it."

"You can't lose," the man snapped back, irritation plainly evident in his voice. "It's nice to know that my friends," he emphasized the word friends, "here in the hospital are all rooting for me."

"See you around, fellow." The ambulance attendant waved, his grin covering his entire face. "Nothing I admire more than a guy with guts—take her easy!"

For many minutes after the ambulance attendant left, the man's heart beat rapidly and his cheeks burned. "What a slimy bastard," he muttered, tightening his fists until they grew numb. "The way he acted, it looked like he's just waiting for me to kick off so he can try and make out with my wife. Everybody in the hospital rooting for me. Probably taking a pool to see how long I'll last. What're the odds on me living till the baby is born?

"Well, you all lose, every goddamn one of you!" He spoke out as if his room were full of people. "All you smartass doctors with your superior ways. All you nice sympathetic people who are so terribly concerned about me. I'll outlive ninety percent of you. I'll live to piss on your graves, you stinking lovers of sickness and death. You all expect me to die. Even my wife expects me to die. The bitch. It would break all your lousy hearts if I walked out of here cured— screw up all your theories, wouldn't it? Well, prepare your- selves for the shock of your lives. This baby is going to throw the rule book away. This kid is not going to let you talk him into giving up."

He lowered his voice. "What a rotten stinking place. Why would anyone want to work in a place like this?" Then in an artificial nasal tone he answered, "To help humanity." The man turned his eyes toward the door, toward the place where the ambulance attendant's head had been. "To help human- ity, shit! That's what you tell yourselves. You work here because you enjoy it. You like playing the game of life and death. Well, I'm 'it.' Try and catch me, you bastards. Maybe you have the rest of them fooled, but you don't fool me."

The man's eyes were still turned toward the door when it opened and his wife walked in. Instead of greeting her, he con- tinued his angry flow of words, but in a louder voice. He acted as if she had been listening to him and understood the reasons for his distress. "They treat you like an infant. Lie to you. Won't tell you what's wrong or what they are doing to you. When you have leukemia, you are supposed to die; it is expected of you—one of the rules of the game. Maybe the rules apply to everybody else. I don't give a damn about everybody else. All I am concerned with is number one, me." The woman stood just inside the door, shocked by her hus- band's angry words, confused as to why they were directed at her.

"You listen to me," he sputtered, "I will be walking out of this hospital under my own power. You may not believe me, but you listen carefully and in twenty years you can beg my pardon for not believing. I am walking out of this hospital and I won't be coming back. I know how to destroy this thing inside me. I told you yesterday and you pretended to accept what I said—I was watching you; I saw your eyes. Well, I've had from yesterday to today to try it out. It works." The man's voice abruptly changed to one of sincere pleading. "It really works. Last night I risked my life to test it and I'm still here. I need your help, yours and a couple of others. I need more mind power. That is why it's so important that you understand and believe me."

The man abruptly stopped speaking and glared at his wife, waiting for her to reply. "You risked your life?" she asked hesitantly.

"Last night I had to find out so I took the chance. If I had lost . . ." the man shrugged his shoulders.

"You feel better, don't you?" The woman was uneasy and tried to change the subject.

"You see," the man chortled, "I told you it was working. You can tell that I'm better. All you had to do was look at me and you knew."

"You sound different, a little stronger." The woman cocked her head to one side while she examined her husband's face. "And your face, it has more color. I'm so glad, honey, so very, very glad."

"Now listen," the man waved his hand impatiently, "most of the people here in the hospital cannot be expected to help. They're convinced I have to die and that is that. All the arguments in the world won't change their minds. I figure I need three more besides myself. I cannot know for sure, but three feels about right."

"I don't . . ." the woman started to say, but was immediately interrupted.

"You don't understand." The man tried to control the excitement that rose in waves and caused his limbs to quiver. "I knew you weren't really paying attention yesterday—all right, I don't care. Just listen carefully."

183

The woman nodded her head rapidly several times. The man's excitement was beginning to have an effect upon her.

"This damn leukemia can be licked if I concentrate every bit of my mind's strength into my body, into my bones and flesh and blood—everywhere. We know how powerful the human mind is. The doctors themselves will tell you that. The trick is to harness that energy. When I first discovered this theory, I thought it might be possible to work it all by myself. I'm not one hundred percent convinced that I couldn't pull it off alone, but I probably can't." The man stopped speaking and cleared his throat several times.

"I still don't quite understand," the woman murmured, half to herself.

"If you will only give me a chance," the man growled, still trying to lubricate his throat. Then slightly ashamed, he mumbled, "I'm sorry, I didn't mean to jump on you. What I am trying to say—as I talk about it, it gets even clearer in my mind—what I mean is, I doubt if I can produce enough energy myself. The reason I don't think I can is, first of all, I'm sick and weak. If I were well, it might be a different story, but if I were well, I wouldn't need to. That's the first reason.

"The second reason I think I need help is I realized other sick people must have thought about using the power of their minds to get well. Over the years some of them must have discovered what I did. Why weren't they successful? I asked myself that question. Then I decided they failed because they probably needed help. Maybe a few asked for help but nobody would believe them. Some people may have said, 'yes, sure,' like you did yesterday, but they were only humoring the patients. Don't think I haven't thought through every part of this theory. It's possible that when certain individuals hear about what I am doing and don't believe me, they may somehow draw off part of my energy. I'm not saying that I believe this, but if I want to succeed I have to think of every

184

possibility. I may have made a mistake mentioning anything to the resident; now that I think about it, I'm sure I was wrong."

"Do you think he would really try to work against you?" The woman, by her question, demonstrated that for the moment she accepted her husband's theory.

"He is convinced that I have to die. He wants me to last until after the baby, but then he expects me to turn up my toes. Nothing I say can convince him. All he believes in is medicines and things like that."

"How do you know you need three?" The woman felt tiny needle pricks of doubt. She listened to her own words and they sounded foolish.

"I can't be sure," the man dropped his voice, "I really don't know if three is the correct number." His voice was reduced to a whisper. "Might be safer if I had four . . . No!" He raised his voice. "Three is the correct number. Something inside tells me three is enough. If we can get an extra, so much the better, but three is enough."

"Don't you think you're getting too excited?" The woman suddenly grew distressed at her husband's words as she realized that she did not believe them. She felt dishonest and wanted to get away. "The doctor warned me not to get you excited or stay too long."

"I'll stop in a minute." The man tried to control the almost hysterical note that was creeping into his voice. "If I can line up three people we can do it tomorrow. We'll decide on a time and I will put everything I have into forcing my mind down into my body. At the same time you and the other two will concentrate all your thoughts on getting inside my body. If we can coordinate, one time may be all I need. Four minds turned on full blast—wham!"

The woman stood up and started edging towards the door. "I better go now."

"I think I can count on the orderly," the man mused, scarcely aware of what his wife was doing. "You, the orderly —I need one more. By tomorrow I'll be set."

After opening the door, the woman hesitated. "I'll do everything I can," she forced herself to say. "I'll be back this afternoon and we can talk some more."

The man nodded at his wife as she left the room, then immediately went back to his rumination.

# 39

A few minutes after his wife left, the man's thinking was interrupted by the appearance of a new visitor. His first reaction was one of irritation since the newcomer was a stranger and he resented the interruption. Then recognizing the other's uniform to be that of an intern, the man sighed, temporarily abandoning his thoughts as he waited to be examined.

"Thank goodness all the patients don't look as distressed to see me as you do. I'd give up medicine and start driving a cab if they did. You probably don't remember me, but I was in the emergency room when you were brought in." The intern pulled over one of the chairs and sat down next to the patient's bed.

"You going to examine me?" the man asked in a dull voice.

"No, you can rest easy. You have been peered at and poked enough." The intern grinned as he spoke. "I just came by to say hello. I'll leave the examinations to others."

"Thanks for coming by." The man forced himself to be polite. He felt his energy fading and his eyes growing heavy and he wanted to do more thinking before he fell asleep, yet he was unable to make himself ask the other to leave.

"You look like you have been deep in thought. Did I interrupt something?"

"That's OK." The man was softened by the doctor's friendly manner. "I was thinking," he yawned, "about a theory I've been working on." His eyes started to shut.

"What kind of theory?"

"A way to cure this damn disease," the man mumbled.

"I'd be very interested in hearing your theory." The intern leaned toward the patient, gently placing a hand on his shoulder.

The man's eyes opened a little. "You want to hear my theory?"

"I have always believed that there are many things doctors can learn from patients. I would like very much to hear your ideas."

The man's eyes opened wide. For the moment sleep was not important. "I have been working on a theory—how to use the power of your mind to cure certain diseases."

The intern nodded to show that he was listening carefully.

"In spite of what you doctors say," the man spat out the word doctors, "I have figured out how to beat this lousy case of leukemia."

The intern kept nodding his head and from time to time made appropriate throat noises as the man explained his theory. When he was finally done, the doctor muttered, "Very interesting, very interesting."

"Sounds good, doesn't it, doc?" The man's cheeks showed patches of red color.

"Very interesting," the young doctor repeated. "We still know very little about leukemia—why some people contract it while others don't. You've done enough thinking and talking for a little while." He patted the patient's arm. "Go to sleep. I'll stick my head in and say hello tomorrow."

"I need three others," the man said shyly, embarrassed to ask the intern directly to help.

The intern, pretending not to understand the meaning of

the man's words, said as he got up to leave, "You go to sleep ... I promise to come by again tomorrow."

The man whispered, "OK," then closed his eyes. The intern's unspoken rejection produced a heaviness in his brain. The heaviness ached and suddenly he felt lonely.

"The way he listened I thought he understood what I was saying." Despite his fatigue, the man was wide awake and ideas kept forming in his brain. "He looked like he agreed with me and then pretended not to understand what I wanted. Maybe he needs a little time to turn it over in his mind. Maybe when he comes by tomorrow ..." The man abruptly cut himself off. "The hell with him," he muttered, "they are all the same. Humor the patient, that's what they do. To them we are little children. Sometimes they listen to us, but it's like most people when they listen to children—they really don't pay attention. They can't believe that the child might have something important to say, that he might know more than the adult about some things. I'm a damn fool if I waste any more time on doctors."

The man turned his eyes toward the window. He had been too busy to enjoy the rich yellow light pouring into his room. "The way the sun is shining, the sky must be clear," he thought. "It will be good to walk out of this place and look up at the sun. I'll look until my eyes water—no, I better not, it might affect my vision. I'll just stand on the sidewalk and let the sun shine on my head." He smiled as he saw himself dressed in street clothes, bathed in sunlight. "Like an angel," he murmured.

He closed his eyes trying to see the image more clearly. He was golden and the sun warmed his body, warmed him in a way different from anything he had ever experienced. "My bones will be warm again," he sighed. "My fingers and toes— all of me will be strong and well."

Between the pulses of delicious thought, insidiously,

189

without the man being aware of what was happening, icy bits of doubt started to form. He forced his mind to concentrate on the golden image, but the man looked less and less like himself and the gold dimmed. Slowly at first, like drops of corrosive acid, tiny scraps of suspicion began to dissolve his belief in his theory. Then in a rush the man was overwhelmed by doubt. "You have been fooling yourself." He shook his head from side to side trying to say no. "You are a child and you have been playing a childish game, making believe you know how to get well. The doctors treat you like a child because that is how you have been acting."

The man lifted his head a few inches off the pillow, moving it in the direction of the light-filled window. "Don't, don't," he mumbled as the cruel thoughts beat in his brain. "If you don't believe," he groaned, "you are finished—dead." He pushed himself up a little more, then rested on his unsteady arm. "Don't let yourself go just because a couple of doctors won't understand." His arm gave way and his head dropped back on the pillow. He could feel himself tottering at the edge of a great dark hole. It yawned wide, waiting for him to fall in and be sucked into blackness. The man struggled to escape the hole.

"Remember, when they said you couldn't hit that bottle and how they laughed?" The man dragged his mind back from the pit to a summer night two years before he got married. He held his mind on the memory, fighting to eliminate all other thoughts. For months he had been spending time in a vacant lot developing his throwing arm. For a quarter of an hour before going to work and for a like amount of time after work he had practiced pitching rocks at tin cans. His skill had developed to a point where after one or two preliminary throws to gauge the distance, he could hit the targets time after time, even when they were placed as much as 100 feet away. He was very proud of his skill.

That night he was standing in front of a movie house after the show with a number of acquaintances. Approximately 100 feet away, sitting on a sawhorse next to a partially completed building, was an empty glass jar. Several young men picked up stones scattered from the construction site and skimmed them at the jar. He remembered the satisfaction he experienced watching the others throw wide of the mark. Impulsively he offered to bet anyone a dollar that he could break the jar within three tries. Every boy in the group wanted to bet and they started taunting him with names of various great baseball pitchers as if he were a combination of them all.

The man remembered he felt then like he felt now. A terrible chilling doubt rose up from his stomach and his confidence grew less and less. The girls stood silent, looking at him, waiting for him to throw. He wanted to run away and never see any of them again. The hard amber light from the street lamps threw slanting black shadows on the sidewalk. The half-finished building looked like a heap of gigantic bones. The boys were laughing and pointing, the girls grinning and waiting.

The first stone struck the sawhorse just to the left of the jar. The second broke the jar into several pieces, leaving only the base still standing. The third stone shattered the base. The crunch of breaking glass as the second and third stones struck was the sweetest sound he'd ever heard. For several minutes he found it hard to catch his breath as his friends playfully punched him in the arm and asked why he didn't try playing professional baseball. He trembled with excitement and wanted to remain there forever.

"Remember how you felt," he told himself. "You wanted to run away. You knew you could hit it, but because they said you couldn't, because they said no, you began to doubt also. It's the same thing now!" The man lifted his hand and rubbed it over his perspiration-covered face. The hand was cold and it trembled slightly. "You almost threw everything away," he murmured. "You were ready to forget all the things you worked out—what a fool." Impulsively he slapped his face with his hand. It stung and he slapped his face again. "Fool!" he muttered, then slapped it a third time.

The blows made him dizzy and left him with drawing pains in his head and neck. "It serves you right. Anyone who is ready to forget everything he knows just because every last person in the world doesn't agree with him deserves to have a little pain." The man smiled, enjoying his burning cheeks and the ache in his head and neck. "You do that again," he warned himself, "your face will be so sore you will think you were hit in the head with a baseball bat. You expect your wife and others to cooperate and you almost flake out yourself." He started to rub his still-smarting face, but his hand went limp and he plunged into an exhausted sleep.

# 40

The woman hesitated in the entranceway to the waiting room. She searched the room with her eyes, then went out to the front gate of the hospital and looked up and down the street. With a sigh she shrugged her shoulders and returned to the waiting room, taking a chair close to the door. She stared down at the tile floor, shifting her position a little so that each of her feet was the same distance away from a particular broken tile. Her feet looked large and ugly in their practical heavy brown oxfords and her abdomen felt mountainous.

"Were you looking for me?" the fat woman asked, placing her puffy hand on the other's shoulder.

The woman's head jerked up. "You startled me! How did you know?"

The fat woman started to smile but instead her mouth sagged open. "I knew," she mumbled; then in a more distinct but expressionless voice she said, "My husband died. This morning just before sunrise he died. I was sleeping at home when he went."

"Oh!" The woman sucked in her breath, grabbing the other's cold damp hand with both of hers. "I'm sorry," she whispered, "very, very sorry." Tears began to form in her eyes. "Can I do anything?"

"I was sleeping when he kicked the bucket." The fat woman allowed the other to continue to hold her hand. "I went home and went to bed. I knew he'd be gone by morning. I couldn't do him any good. They had him shot full of dope. They asked if I would let them perform an autopsy." The fat woman chuckled, but her face remained expressionless. "I told them they could cut him up and use him for dog meat. You should have seen the doctor's face. Who wants a dead body?" She pulled back her hand and put it behind her. "This will be the last time I'll see you." She nodded at the seated woman. "Are you going to help your husband?" she suddenly asked.

"How did you know?" The younger woman shrank back in her chair. "Have you been spying on me?"

The fat woman grinned, her brown teeth showing between her parted lips. "All you ever talked about is how you helped make him sick. If that's how you feel, the least you can do is try to make him well."

"I was just talking," the woman murmured. "I never really believed it. I was upset and let myself say anything."

"You didn't know what you were saying." The fat woman cackled. "That's a good one. Now you have an excuse not to help him." She began to shake with laughter. "She doesn't know how the words got into her mouth. Now I've heard everything."

"My husband thinks he can get well," the woman said quickly, then looked at the other's face, waiting for her reaction.

"But you don't, is that it?"

"He has leukemia. No one can get well who has leukemia."

"That's right. That's right. You're absolutely correct. No one can get well with leukemia. So he thinks he can get well?" the fat woman grinned again, exposing her teeth to their roots, "what does he know? He's doomed, finished. Nothing you

194

can do for him. Like I told you from the start, he brought it on himself. He fixed you good. In a little while he will be dead, nice and comfortably dead, and you will be left. You and your baby. You and me, we go on by ourselves; they, they don't know anything, the sons of bitches."

The woman felt her body tighten with anger, then a wave of horror swept through her as she realized that her anger was not directed toward the fat woman, but at her husband.

After the fat woman left, the woman sagged in her chair, her eyes half-closed. "I hate this place," she whimpered to herself. "I'd give anything if I never had to come here again. Day after day," she moaned. "I wish it were over one way or the other." As if it were a reflex movement, she jerked her hand up and covered her mouth. "You should be ashamed," she scolded herself. "You never change; all you ever think about is yourself." She allowed her hand to fall to her lap. Her eyes, following her hand, focused on her swollen belly. "Coming to the hospital day after day is not doing the baby any good." She began to defend herself. "It's not fair to take a chance with a helpless infant; suppose I pick up an infection or something?

"Maybe in a few more days he'll be well enough to come home. He looked better this morning." The image of her husband lying in the hospital bed floated through her mind. "I wonder if he was afraid of becoming a father," she mused. "Maybe marriage and having the responsibility of a child were too much for him and that's why he got sick. If we had never met, he might be well and happy instead of ..." The woman sighed several times, allowing herself to sink into melancholy. "I can't blame myself," she uttered softly. "Just one of those things. I wish there was something I could do for him." For a moment she thought about his theory. "I'm glad he has something to hold onto," she decided. "It must be very hard to know you are going to die. The least I can do is go along with his theory, poor baby. Let him believe I'm convinced. I wish there really was a way I could help him."

The woman's thoughts were scattered as she sensed someone standing behind her chair. Somehow she knew it was a man and she tensed. Afraid that she might be in for another session with the ambulance attendant, she pretended not to be aware of the other's presence, keeping her eyes focused directly ahead.

"Have you been up to see your husband yet?"

The woman quickly shifted position and looked up into the face of the family doctor. She smiled with relief when she saw who it was. "I spent a few minutes with him before. I try to visit him twice a day."

"Good girl." The doctor nodded his head in approval. "You are the best possible medicine for him. He's a brave boy, but he needs help to keep his spirits up."

"How is he? He looked better when I saw him."

"I was just on my way up when I spotted you. The way you were sitting—I decided a friendly word or two would be welcome. Is it getting you down?"

The woman started to shake her head, then shrugged her shoulders instead. "Maybe a little bit. I wish he could come home. I don't like this place."

"Just be patient." The doctor spoke soothingly. "He is being given the best treatment possible. With a little luck he may be ready to leave in a week or two."

"A week or two," the woman sighed, "then how long before he has to come back?"

"That, my dear, nobody knows. My advice to you is to enjoy your husband as much as possible, taking each day as it comes. His state of mind will play a big part in how long he remains at home and you can do a great deal to help keep him from becoming upset."

"The mind does have an important effect, doesn't it?"

"More than even we doctors know. The human mind has capabilities that we have not yet begun to explore."

"Do you think it's possible that even a fatal disease can be cured through the strength of the mind?" The woman spoke softly, but there was a great urgency in her voice.

"Anything is possible," the doctor answered cautiously. "I said nothing about being cured. What I said is that the mind can have a powerful effect on the body and that there are many things about the brain no one understands."

"My husband has a theory. He is convinced that he can get well. That's all he talked about the last two times I saw him."

"Many patients with—ah," the doctor hesitated, "many patients who know their days are numbered do what your husband is doing. They convince themselves that they will somehow prove to be the exception, the one case in a million. Some just refuse to believe the diagnosis and behave as if they were suffering from a temporary indisposition. If a patient knows the facts and then either cannot or will not face them, I never try to force him. Each of us must be allowed to handle our crises in our own way."

"But my husband's theory is based on the same thing you just said." The woman spoke carefully, trying to organize her thoughts as she went along.

"I said?" The doctor touched his chest with his index finger.

"About the mind. He thinks that if he can concentrate all the strength in his brain, turn it inside into his body, he can destroy the disease. When he tells you about it, you can almost be convinced." The woman hesitated, then responding to the interested expression on the doctor's face, continued. "He said he tested it out last night, took a chance—he didn't explain how—and proved that his theory worked." The woman lowered her voice almost to a whisper. "He looked better this morning . . ."

197

"You didn't argue with him, did you? Of course you didn't." The doctor patted the woman on her shoulder. "Let him believe whatever he wants. Let him have hope. We all need to believe in something. That is what religion is all about. With him it's a belief in himself, David facing a Goliath as tall as a mountain. Let him think he is David."

"He said he needs help. He has to have others who believe in him concentrate their minds, add their power to his."

"Help him, by all means help him, whatever he says. What possible harm can it do and if it makes him happier even for a little while, so much the better."

"Do you think there is a chance he might be right?" The woman turned her face upward and looked deep into the doctor's eyes. "Do you think that there is even a tiny chance—if he can concentrate his mind and if he has others to help?"

The doctor's eyes shifted away, then he rolled them up toward the ceiling. "If your husband asked me that question," the doctor chose his words carefully, "I would probably answer yes. I would answer yes, just as I would not deny him the relief of a narcotic if he were in pain. If I could make him more comfortable by telling him a little untruth, particularly when I know what answer he really wants, I would not hesitate to administer a proper dose of fabrication. But right now I am not talking to your husband. You asked me a direct question; you deserve a direct answer. There is not the slightest chance your husband's plan will work. He is suffering from an incurable disease. All we can hope for is a temporary prolongation of life, but," the doctor laid his hand gently on the woman's head, "if he has peace of mind, that in itself is an immensely valuable thing. If his mind is at rest, he will enjoy those days he has left. Help him any way you can."

After he left the woman, all the way to the patient's room the doctor thought about what had been said. During the course of their conversation he was confident that he was playing the role of supportive family doctor to its ultimate perfection. As he moved through the hospital corridors, he was not so certain.

"What makes you so cocksure of yourself?" he muttered. "Would it have hurt if you left her a glimmer of hope? Would you be willing to swear on your own life that somehow that kid might not work a miracle? You sounded a little like God back there."

# 41

The man's eyes were blinded by the glare of the footlights. Squinting, he tried to force his vision through the shimmering wall of light. Out front he could hear the rustlings of hundreds of people. The air was dense with human odor and he knew that the theater was packed. No one else was on stage. He glanced to the right and left, but the wings were obscured by a gauze-like silvery haze. There was no scenery and no props except for a microphone suspended by a wire. He looked up; the ceiling was not visible. It might have been twenty feet high or a hundred or a thousand. There was no way of telling.

Suddenly the audience settled down, the rustlings, whispers and coughs faded and the theater grew absolutely still. "I wish I could see them," the man thought, "see their faces, know who they are." The audience waited and the man knew he had to begin.

"I wish I could see your faces." His words were picked up by the amplifying system and boomed through the theater. "If someone would dim these lights, it would make it a lot easier." He waited; the lights continued to blaze and the audience remained silent. "I have never spoken to a group before," the man lifted his hands palms upward, "I didn't know you couldn't see the audience when you're on stage." He grinned foolishly, then scratched his head. He tried to remember why he was there and wondered what the people expected him to say.

"I don't know why I am here, but I appreciate your coming to hear me. I really should be dead by now." The man felt foolish and twisted his body in embarrassment. "I guess that is why I'm here. You must all be doctors wanting to learn how I did it." The man assumed an oratorical pose with one hand raised in the air—his history books had been full of pictures of men in just such a pose. "Gentlemen, up until recently a dread disease raged inside my body. I was a victim of leukemia and was condemned to a lingering but certain death."

The man liked the sound of his voice and forced it down into his chest to give it added resonance. "In defiance of all medical knowledge, I developed a system to harness the greatest source of power on earth—the human mind. I refused to accept my sentence of death and used all the strength I possessed to hunt down the particles of disease within my body. Nothing could withstand the burning power of my brain. Gentlemen, we are born to live, not to die. Death is a horrible accident. I hate and despise death. Together we must travel all over the world. I will go with you as a living example. Gentlemen, we can destroy death. Will you join with me to teach the ways of life?"

The man bowed from his waist and waited for the applause. "We can destroy death!" he shouted, his voice rolling through the theater. "Will you join with me?"

Suddenly the glaring footlights faded and the theater was flooded with light from above. The man looked out at the audience. They shuffled silently down the aisles, leaving the theater through every exit.

"Wait!" he shouted. "Won't any of you join me?" Not one person turned his head. The silent lines kept moving away. He was about to jump off the stage and run after the disappearing people when suddenly he noticed that they all wore black.

The man opened his eyes and stared up at the face of the family physician. "They were all undertakers. The lights blinded my eyes and I couldn't see them." The man's throat was tight with horror. "Undertakers, and they came to hear me."

"You were asleep," the doctor spoke soothingly. "You were dreaming. It was nothing but a dream."

"I thought they were doctors," the man moaned. "I told them how I learned to destroy death. I asked them to join with me to teach the ways of life. Them!"

"That's all right." The doctor started blotting the perspiration on the sick man's forehead. "Try and put it out of your mind. It was only a dream."

"I thought they were doctors and they were undertakers," the man said softly. "What a terrible mistake."

"I saw your wife down in the lobby." The doctor lifted the patient's head as he readjusted the pillow. "If she gets any bigger," he chuckled, "she will have to carry her belly around in a wheelbarrow. What do you want, a boy or a girl?"

"It doesn't matter," the man mumbled, still groggy from sleep.

"Have you decided on any names?"

"Names? I don't care. Names don't mean anything. All I care about is that the baby be strong and healthy." The man's eyes opened wide. "There is nothing I want more in the whole world than that baby. Before I got sick, it didn't matter. I kind of felt it belonged to my wife. But now," the man's eyes lit up and he smiled, "I think about it all the time.

"I want to raise my kid and watch it grow." The man's eyes were filmed with moisture. "I want to teach it how to talk, go together on picnics and hikes through the woods. I'm going to raise my kid right, I swear it."

"Now, now, you're getting yourself excited." The doctor hesitated, searching his mind for a suitable topic of conversation. The man's hopes for his unborn child were unnerving. "Have you been moving your bowels regularly?" the doctor asked; it was the best that he could do.

The man's face took on a vacant expression. "My bowels? I don't know. I don't remember."

"Some patients have difficulty adjusting to a bedpan." The doctor patted the patient's hand. "I must ask the nurse how you have been doing."

"You don't believe that I will live to raise my kid," the man said softly. "I talk about my baby and you talk about my shit."

The doctor's face burned with embarrassment and for several seconds he was unable to reply. "There is no need to speak to me in that manner, young man." He assumed his most severe professional tone. "As a physician I am concerned with each of my patients' well-being. The various bodily functions are matters that must be checked regularly."

"I don't give a damn if you believe me or not. You wouldn't understand if I explained it, so I won't even try." The man shut his eyes and turned his head away. "I'll keep an accurate record of how many times I crap," he muttered into his pillow. "Come by tomorrow and I'll give you the good news."

A little more abruptly than was his wont, the doctor released the patient's hand and walked out of the room.

# 42

After the doctor left the room the man continued to lie with his face partially buried in the pillow. "He didn't mean any harm." He was sorry he had been rude to the doctor. "I'll apologize next time I see him."

The idea of having incurred the enmity of the doctor made him uneasy. "Doesn't do you a damn bit of good getting people mad at you, especially doctors. You can use every bit of help you can get. I'll tell the nurse to tell him I'm sorry I was rude," he decided. The image of flashing lightning flickered in his mind. "You don't stand up in the middle of a field during a storm and make yourself a target. You don't look for trouble with doctors."

He thought of buzzing for the nurse to convey his apologies right away, but restrained himself. Instead, he moved his head back into a more comfortable position.

"So he doesn't believe I'll live to raise my kid. You didn't expect him to, did you? At least I didn't panic like with the other doctor; that's progress. I wonder if it will be a boy or a girl. Big as she is it might be twins." The man grinned. "I hope it's twins." His grin grew larger. "I wouldn't be mad if she had triplets. Boy, no one would get any sleep. Up all night giving them bottles, changing diapers, what a mess.

Might have to get an extra job on weekends. Triplets," he began to chuckle, "wouldn't that be a bitch. Have my entire family at one time. Three would be just about enough."

The man interrupted his reverie, deliberately turning his thoughts onto himself. "You really do feel better," he spoke out loud, an undertone of wonder in his voice. "Not much pain." He mentally checked each of his arms and legs. "Stomach hasn't acted up in quite a while." He cautiously probed his abdomen. The skin was tender from the scratches, but the insides were not overly sensitive. "And you're feisty as hell," he laughed softly, "ready to quarrel with everyone in the hospital. I'll bet old slime cola never had anyone talk to him like that before."

He pulled his arms up, placing them behind his head. They were stiff and his shoulders ached a little, but he scarely noticed the discomfort. The air soothed the exposed underside of his arms and felt good as it dried the perspiration in his armpits. "Except for this feeling of weakness," he thought, "I don't feel any worse than when I've had a slight cold. A little achy, a little stiff, but that's all. I really am getting better. All that thinking I've been doing is having an effect. Tomorrow I knock it out for good."

The man ignored a tiny irritating thought that tugged at the edge of his consciousness. The possibility that his improved state might be only a remission, he refused to consider. Just feeling better had seemed important several days earlier, but now it was not enough, not nearly enough.

Several minutes passed before the man was aware his wife was in the room. He had drifted off into a light sleep without realizing it, and the woman had been careful not to disturb him. She was gazing toward the window when he opened his eyes and for several minutes did not notice that he was no longer sleeping.

He looked at her with the window light washing her hair,

illuminating her tranquil face. He saw her hands laced together resting on her abdomen. He gazed tenderly at her swollen body. He felt as if a stream of warm milk were flowing through his body. He wanted to reach out and draw her close, to feel her skin against his, to lay his head between her breasts and hear nothing except the beating of her heart.

She turned her head and their eyes met and she smiled. "You're awake," she said softly, "and you have been watching me." The man nodded. "Why didn't you let me know you were awake?"

"I just wanted to look at you for a while. It was nice to open my eyes and find you there."

"You're very sweet," she whispered, lowering her eyes. "If they didn't have those rules about wearing a mask and not getting too close, I'd come over and give you a great big hug."

"The heck with the rules. Rules were made to be broken." The man lifted his arms from behind his head and held them open.

She started to get up, hesitated, then shook her head several times. "I'd never forgive myself if you got sick. The worst thing that can happen is an infection at this time." She sat back down heavily. "I'm sorry, honey, I really am sorry."

"That's all right," the man said in a husky voice, dropping his arms to the bed. "I wouldn't want to get you in trouble."

"It's not me; I don't care a thing for myself." The woman's voice broke as she spoke.

"Forget it. Forget it. It doesn't make any difference. Let's talk about something else."

"How are you feeling, honey?"

"At least you didn't ask me about my bowel movements." Before the words were completely out of his mouth, the man started chuckling. "My bowels seem to be a major topic of interest around this place. That, and will I make it until the baby is born."

"Now, honey," the woman pleaded.

"Don't worry. I'm not one bit upset. I know what's going on, but it doesn't bother me. I think I'll make it my business to come back here one more time. When the baby reaches its first birthday, I'll drop by. It would give me the greatest possible pleasure to stick the baby into their faces and say, 'See?'" The man winked his eye to show his wife he was enjoying himself.

"Before you came in, I was thinking," he hesitated, embarrassed, "about the baby. I was wondering if it will be a boy or a girl. Not that it matters," he quickly added, "but I was wondering. Then I thought maybe it's twins. Even the doctor said you're pretty big." The man's eyes were crinkled with smiles. "Then it came to me. Like a flash."

"What came to you?"

"It's triplets." He started laughing. "Something tells me it's triplets."

"Are you sure it isn't four or even quintuplets?"

"You never know." The man's body shook with laughter. "The doctor said if you get any bigger you will have to carry your belly in a wheelbarrow."

"Now that isn't very nice." The woman pretended to be put out.

"I agree. You are absolutely correct. A wheelbarrow isn't very nice. How about an electric go-cart? I wouldn't want a wife of mine to walk around pushing no clumsy wheelbarrow. Nothing is too good for this family."

"Now you behave."

"I'm just trying to be helpful. But seriously," the man started laughing again, "I'm trying to be dead serious," his laughter made it difficult for him to speak, "I think I can count on triplets. When they're one year old, I'll walk up to everyone here in the hospital and say, "See, see, see!'"

"You are full of beans," the woman joined in with the laughter. "Triplets, the idea. I'd lose my mind. I'd never be able to handle them."

"Don't worry, I'll help."

The woman's mirth was suddenly choked off. "Yes, of course you will." She tried to make her voice sound light, but instead it came out forced. "When a husband and wife work together, things are much easier." She stopped speaking and looked at her husband, then turned her eyes away. He was staring at her with a fixed expression. Several minutes passed while neither one of them spoke.

Finally the man cleared his throat, then cleared it again. The woman kept her eyes averted. "Look at me," he ordered. "I won't bite you. Look at me."

She moved her head a little. She was thankful for the gauze mask. It hid her trembling lips.

"Do I sound crazy?" the man asked in an earnest, quiet voice. "Do you think I'm a loony?" The woman shook her head. "Ask me something," he begged, "ask me anything. Dates, the names of presidents, what year it is—go ahead and ask me."

The woman's eyebrows drew together and she silently shook her head.

"My mind is as clear," the man groped for an appropriate comparison, "is as clear as a diamond. I never was able to think more clearly than I have for the past two days. I know what I am saying. Please believe me."

"I'll try." Suddenly the woman's voice cracked and she started sobbing. "I want to believe you. I do. I do. I do."

"That's all right," the man murmured, "I didn't mean to upset you. That's all right. I'm sorry, baby. It's just that I want you to understand."

"I'll try," she repeated. "Give me another chance. I'll try."

"You see how I'm getting better." The man spoke gently, as if he were addressing a child. "I feel stronger than I did this morning and the pain scarcely bothers me. Doesn't that prove something is happening?"

"You don't look as pale; your eyes are clearer and your voice is more like you used to sound."

"That's just the beginning." The man smiled at his wife. "Nobody ever tried what I'm trying before, not that I know of anyway. It's all new. Most people when they are told they have some incurable disease either believe it or they don't. If they don't believe it, they put it out of their minds and pretend nothing is wrong. Then wham! It's all over. If they do believe it, they either accept what the doctor says and resign themselves to death, or they pray for a miracle or hope for a medical breakthrough.

"I believe it. The doctors say I have leukemia and I believe it. You don't hear me arguing with them, do you? I also believe that leukemia is a disease they don't know how to cure. You see, I'm different from the other patients. You know how I'm different? I'm different because I will not lie back and wait to die or pray for a miracle or hope for a medical breakthrough. I'm fighting it myself, here," the man hit his chest with his fist, "inside me. I have the power in my mind to do part of it, but I need help, your help most of all. This has never been done before. Just think what it will mean when I show them that there is a way to destroy this stinking disease." The man was breathing very rapidly; he paused to catch his breath.

"It sounds so logical," the woman said softly. Then in a louder voice, "It sounds so right."

"Yes, that's it." The man giggled with excitement. "You put your finger on it exactly. It sounds so right. You know how sometimes you know something and everyone says you're

209

wrong. Like you read it somewhere, in a book or the encyclopedia, but you don't remember and you get into an argument and everybody tells you you don't know what you're talking about, and you know as sure as you know your name that you are correct." The woman's eyes sparkled and she kept nodding her head. "They make fun of you, then later you look it up and you were right.

"It's the same thing now. I know I'm right. No point in arguing with them, the doctors especially. If I didn't need help, I wouldn't even try to convince you. A year from now, without me saying a word, you would be convinced. But I can't do it by myself."

Raising her right hand the woman gasped, "I swear I will help you. I understand. I do understand." She got up and ran across the room falling on her knees next to her husband's bed. "I want you to live. I want you. I'll do anything."

The man placed his hand on his wife's head. She grabbed it and pressed it against her cheek. For several minutes she remained crouched by his bed, then still holding his hand she slowly got to her feet. "I'm sorry it took so long and was so hard to make me understand," she murmured. "You don't have to worry about me anymore; just tell me what to do."

"Tomorrow, after I talk to the others. Tomorrow in the morning when you come to see me." The man pulled back his hand. "Better not let them see you this close. No point in taking a chance. The worst thing that could happen would be if they didn't allow you to visit."

The woman walked to the door. Just before opening it she turned back. "By the way," she said, her eyes focused on the floor, "I thought you might want to know," she felt embarrassed and awkward, "I love you."

Before the man had a chance to answer, she was gone. "Oh God," he murmured, tears filling his eyes, "I want to get well. Let me be right. Please, please let me be right."

# 43

Fifteen minutes before he was scheduled to start his shift the orderly knocked gently on the man's door. He had been walking toward the cafeteria for a cup of coffee when he suddenly stopped. A feeling of not having done something important nagged at him, but for several seconds he couldn't remember what. Then, snapping his fingers, he wheeled around and, taking rapid steps, made his way to the man's room.

The man had grown tense waiting and hoping for the orderly to come. Unable to judge the hour, he began to think the other might not show up. The knock on the door startled him though he had been awaiting just such a knock. "I thought you might not be coming." The man's eyes opened wide and they glistened with pleasure as the orderly stepped into the room. "Sure am glad to see you—I figured you had to go to work and didn't have time."

"I came up here first thing," the orderly lied. "I told you I was gonna drop by before going on duty, didn't I?"

The man smiled. "I didn't know what time it was. Seems later. I thought you had started work already. Sure am glad to see you."

The orderly winked. "When I say I'm gonna do something, I do it. Well . . ." He hesitated, about to qualify his statement; then he decided against it and winked again instead. "Do you have a few minutes?" The man's voice carried an edge of anxiety. "I want to talk to you about something very important."

"Sure, I have a few minutes." The orderly pulled one of the chairs over to the foot of the bed and sat down. "You worried? You sound worried. What's bugging you, man?"

"I'm not worried, that's not it. I wanted to talk to you and I guess," the man felt a twinge of embarrassment, "I guess I thought you weren't going to show up. That's all."

The orderly looked at the man tenderly. "Hell, I understand how it is. You got something to say and want to talk to someone. It's no fun lying there all by yourself."

"No. I didn't want to talk to someone. Lots of people keep coming in and out of here. I was waiting for you. I want to talk to you."

"Good enough. Here I am. I got fifteen minutes and it's all yours."

"I've worked out a theory. Maybe you'll find it hard to believe what I'm saying." The man spoke rapidly, clearing his throat constantly. "It's a way to get well—not just better, but well, completely and for good."

Point by point the man carefully detailed his theory. Several times he stopped and nervously looked at the other's face, trying to judge the effect of his words. Each time the man paused the orderly moved forward a few inches in his seat, furrowing his brow to signal his interest and his desire to hear more. When he finished, the man turned his eyes away from the orderly. His heart was pounding very rapidly. Everything he had said suddenly sounded hollow and foolish. An overwhelming desire to sleep swept over him and for a moment his mind drifted.

"You sure have figured it out good. You know what I think?" The orderly leaned part of his weight on the bed, lowering his head until it was almost on a level with the man's. "I think you're a little crazy. Fact of the matter, I think you are some kind of nut." Before the man could react, the orderly chuckled. "Only a crazy man would have the guts to call the doctors wrong. Lying there in your bed, everyone telling you you gonna die and you scheming how to beat it. You gotta be crazy."

"You think I'm crazy?" the man asked, unsure if he understood the other correctly.

"Man, I already told you I thought you was crazy. But I didn't say what kind of crazy. Any man that can lie there sick, weak as a kitten, hurting, with all kinds of needles going in and out of his body, and figure like you do is my kind of crazy."

In a whisper, afraid of the answer he might get, the man asked, "Do you think it will work?" He held his breath. His insides trembled.

"I know it will work. I ain't putting you on." The orderly looked directly into the man's eyes. "I never heard nothing like what you said before in my life. Right here," he placed his hand on his chest, "inside me, I know you are right. I been around this place five years and I never heard nothing like that before. Never."

The man lifted his torso up a few inches; he was quivering and his eyes looked as if they might burst from his head. "You're not putting me on?" he asked in an almost hysterical voice.

"If I thought you was wrong, I wouldn't say anything. I might not tell you I didn't believe you, wouldn't be no point in upsetting you. But, man, I wouldn't fool you, not about something like this."

The man was almost convinced but wanted one final bit of confirmation. "How about before? Before I knew what was wrong with me. You tried to fool me then—like all the rest."

"That was different. Before, you didn't know. Nobody wanted to worry you. As long as you didn't know, what could it hurt making you feel better?"

The man allowed himself to sink back into the bed. "If you help me," he spoke softly, his voice breaking several times, "if you help me . . . I'll never . . . never forget you. Not if I live a hundred years."

"That's OK," the orderly murmured, turning his face away for a moment. "Nothing I'd rather see than you prove them doctors wrong. You can count on me one hundred and one percent."

"You know," the man spoke in a soft, almost childlike voice, "I have scarcely had any pain all day, not even when they changed the sheets."

"You look a hell of a lot better than when I first saw you. When I wheeled you in here, you was a pretty sick boy."

"What I told you, it's already working. When you brought me here, I was a mess. Now . . . I've felt lots worse when I had a cold. Except for being weak, I could get up right now and go home."

"You like to fish?" the orderly asked. The man hesitated, then nodded his head a little. "When you get well, if you can get away from the Mrs., we'll take off for a couple of days, find us a good fast stream and see if we can snag some trout. Ain't nothing I like better than fresh-caught trout dipped in cracker meal and fried all nice and crispy."

"I only been fishing a couple, three times, and never for trout." The man sounded apologetic.

"Leave it up to me. I got plenty extra tackle. In an hour or two under instruction from the master," the orderly made an exaggerated gesture of patting himself on the shoulder, "you can learn to cast a fly with the best of them."

"It would be nice to be in the country," the man sighed. "You don't realize how much you miss trees and grass and earth until you are stuck in a place like this. You know something?" he asked without expecting an answer, "When I get old, when I'm all worn out and tired of living, you know what I'm gonna do? I'm going to say goodbye to everyone I know and go off into the country. I'll walk and walk until I come to some woods; then I'll find a place in the woods where the sun shines through. I'll make a place to lie down from leaves and moss. I'll make it nice and soft where the sun can warm me. Then I'll lie down and rest my head on my arm. Away from everyone, on the ground with trees all around and the sun shining down, I'll go to sleep and sleep forever."

"Jesus Christ," the orderly whispered, "that's what we all should do when our time comes—go to sleep and sleep forever."

"You and me," the man spoke, his eyes swimming in happy tears, "we'll go fishing. And after we fish and you show me how, after we cook supper and eat as much as we want, we'll lie out under the stars and talk about things. We'll let the campfire burn down low until it glows red just enough to keep us warm. We will talk about the time we were together here in the hospital and how I was so weak I couldn't even sit up, and we'll poke the fire and make the sparks jump and we'll laugh about all the things that happened in the hospital, then look up at the stars until we feel tiny as ants."

"Man, I'm ready to go right now." The orderly smiled, closing his eyes for several seconds. "The way you talk, I can smell the wood burning and feel that clean air on my face." He leaned all the way forward taking hold of the sick man's hand. "Let's shake on it. Soon as you get better, I mean soon as you get well, we got a date." He squeezed the limp cold hand.

"We got a date," the man murmured. "Don't forget."

"I won't forget, man. Don't you forget." With a rough, almost painful squeeze of his hand, the orderly jumped to his

215

feet. He started toward the door, then stopped. "You can count on me," he promised. "Whenever you're ready, just let me know. See you tomorrow."

The man's hand tingled for several minutes after the orderly left. Without realizing what he was doing, he lifted it, flexed the fingers several times, then laid it on his cheek.

# 44

The woman lay in the dark of her bedroom settling her body for sleep. All the way home from the hospital she had thought about her husband. For the first time since his illness, he felt like the man with whom she had lived. As she prepared supper, she unconsciously set the table for two, then realizing what she had done, smiled and left the second place undisturbed. Lying there in the dark she allowed herself to imagine what it would be like to have him back.

"It will be months before his strength returns. I'll make sure he gets into bed right after supper. He'll need lots of sleep. It will be extra hard when the baby comes." She smiled and gently stroked her abdomen. "When he gets strong, we'll go for walks; he can push the carriage and I'll look in all the shop windows." She saw the reflection of her husband and herself in the glass of a store window. Between them was a shiny baby carriage. The man stood straight and tall and he was laughing.

"Everybody will stop and look at the baby," she whispered. "They will say how much the baby looks like each of us . . ." She was about to continue with her fantasy when the laughing figure in the plate glass window suddenly stopped laughing and started to weep. She grabbed the covers of her bed and pulled them up over her face. Then with a convulsive gasp she burst out crying. "My poor, poor, sweet husband," she sobbed. "I'd do anything to keep you alive."

She saw the man lying white-faced in the hospital bed. "I want to believe you," she moaned, rocking herself back and forth in the bed. "I want you to live; I do, I do. I tried to believe you. I really did." She turned her face into the pillow and cried until, overcome by exhaustion, she fell asleep.

The woman walked down a street. Trees lined the sidewalk at precisely measured intervals. They looked strange. All the leaves and twigs had been clipped so that each tree was a mass of thick bare limbs ending in ugly knobs. Not a speck of green was on any tree.

The day was warm. It was spring and had been spring for a long time. The woman walked down the street pushing a baby carriage; its wheels rolled silently on their rubber tires and the carriage moved with scarcely more than the pressure of her finger. She was the only one on the street. The houses on both sides were empty and dark. Not a face showed from any window, not a curtain fluttered. No vehicles moved on the pavement. As far as the eye could see in either direction there was no movement. She walked along, proud of the sparkle of the chrome-trimmed carriage, proud of the silk smooth infant sleeping inside. She would walk all day. Her feet felt as if they were tipped with fluffy cotton and her body bubbled with life.

Around the corner came an automobile. It was filled with plump babies; the fat woman drove. The car rushed past, then skidded to a halt. Curls of acrid smoke rose from the wheels and ugly black streaks of burnt rubber showed on the roadway. Inside the automobile the babies were all scrambled together, little arms and legs intertwined, the whole mass crying in desperate infant terror.

The fat woman reached behind her and grabbed a baby. "Here, this is what you wanted." She opened the door and tossed the infant out onto the pavement. With the door still partially open the automobile sped away and disappeared around a corner.

The baby lay where it had fallen some fifty feet from the woman. Its body was twisted like that of a discarded doll. The woman rushed down the street leaving her carriage unattended. She picked up the infant. Its body was soft and warm. She lifted it and peered at its face. It was the haggard white face of her husband. "Oh no!" she gasped. The baby fell from her hands onto the pavement. She whirled around and the carriage was gone. She began to scream, "Where is my baby, where is my baby?" The words echoed up and down the street but no one came and no one answered.

"Where is my baby?" The words tore at her throat and their echoes mocked her. She looked down and saw the infant she had dropped crawling like a dying lizard toward her, its tiny bruised limbs pushing it slowly along the sidewalk. "Get away, get away!" she shrieked. Then crazy with terror, she kicked the dying creature.

The woman sat bolt upright in her bed. The infant in her womb thrashed, kicking and hammering at the wall of her body. She gasped lungful after lungful of air, trying to drive away the horror of the dream. For many minutes the unborn infant continued its agitation. Finally, as the woman brought herself under control, the child within her gradually lessened its movements until at last it was asleep.

The woman settled herself back in the bed but was afraid to close her eyes. She lay there staring into darkness and waited.

219

# 45

Despite his efforts to remain awake until he had a chance to speak to the male nurse, the man fell asleep. Several times during the early part of the night the nurse peeked in, saw the patient resting comfortably, and left without entering. When shortly after midnight the nurse entered the room to take his pulse, the portion of the mind that never sleeps brought the sick man back to full consciousness.

"Shish," the nurse whispered, "go back to sleep. I'll be finished in a minute."

"Got to talk to you," the man mumbled. His mouth felt hot and dry. "Been waiting to talk to you."

"Not now, you go back to sleep; we'll talk in the morning." The nurse made an entry on the chart and started toward the door.

"It's important." The man forced the words to come out clearly. "It'll only take a few minutes."

"Now, I don't want you to get yourself all worked up." The nurse remained standing next to the door. "I can only spend a few minutes; what is it?"

"I want to talk to you." The man hesitated, licking his dry lips with the tip of his tongue, unsure of how to begin. "I 'specially want to talk to you because of the way you treat me, not like the rest, like you are my friend."

"Thank you," the nurse's eyes crinkled, "I'm glad you feel that way. We are friends."

"I need help." The man wished that the nurse wouldn't stand next to the door—it felt like any second he might leave. "I have been thinking; every minute I could find, I have been thinking."

"You said you needed help." The nurse's voice contained a trace of impatience. "What kind of help?"

"I figured out a way to get well, to cure myself, and I need your help."

"I'll do anything I can," the nurse answered quickly. "Just let me know what you need and if it is in my power, you can count on me." He took hold of the knob and started to turn it.

"I haven't told you what I worked out. If you can give me another few minutes," the man pleaded.

"I promise I'll help, but I don't have time to listen to any more now. When you are ready, just tell me what you need."

"But it won't be any good unless I have a chance to explain." The man tried to keep his voice from revealing the anxiety he was beginning to feel.

"Sorry, sport, I have to go, but I meant it when I said you can count on me, so you don't have to worry."

The man opened his mouth, but before he could speak, the nurse was gone. "You don't understand," he whispered to the empty room. "Unless you understand, it's no good." He sighed and tried to find a more comfortable position in the bed. His back had begun to ache and the sheets irritated his skin. "Maybe later when he isn't so busy I can try again," he told himself. "I'll just have to be patient."

The man looked up at the burning light in the ceiling; the nurse had forgotten to turn it off. He tried to make believe that the light was the sun. He closed his eyes and kept them directed upwards so that a portion of the brightness filtered through his eyelids.

221

Stimulated by the imaginary sun, he could see himself as a little boy playing in a field. The wild grass grew up to his waist. As he ran through the grass, he held his hands out letting the stalks hit his palms, catching handfuls of fuzz and seeds, tossing them up into the air. His face and hair were coated with pollen and fluff. The stubbly earth stung his bare feet, but not enough to stop his running. The air was thick and hot, rich with the odor of grass and earth. His nose was clogged with dust and he tasted the air as he sucked it into his mouth. He stopped and looked around. He was surrounded by a million miles of waving grass. The sky looked like a great blue cereal bowl turned upside down. He threw himself on the ground, rolling about until he had flattened out a neat burrow. Then lying face up, he stared into the sky. Countless tiny white specks swam before his eyes. It looked as if the sky swarmed with snow white birds.

The moving grass rustled and whispered. Faint scratching sounds could be heard. He laid his ear against the ground and listened. Between the stalks of grass he saw a mouse. It combed its whiskers with its forepaws, then scurried away. He lay perfectly still; only his eyes moved. There were field mice everywhere. If he listened very carefully, he could hear their faint squeaks as they talked to one another. Occasionally one would dart out and come within several inches of his body, then sensing danger, hunch up and race away.

Very carefully he moved his hand out until it lay cupped and ready. He breathed softly keeping his body perfectly still. A mouse poked its nose between two stalks of grass a half a foot away from his arm. It hesitated, its tiny eyes darting in every direction. Then it quickly moved forward, stopping within an inch of his hand. With a sudden sweeping movement he grabbed the little animal and held it tight. It squirmed and wriggled, thrashing and scratching with its tiny legs. He squeezed harder, trying to stop the desperate writhing of the terror-filled creature. It felt as if it would dig into his hand. He squeezed still harder and the movement suddenly stopped.

Very carefully he opened his hand and looked at the little mouse. It lay still, and even when he poked its belly with a bit of twig, it did not move. He laid the mouse on the ground and covered it with earth until its body was completely hidden. Then slowly and sadly he walked out of the field. The sharp stubble caught between his toes and the dust-filled air burned as he breathed.

"Poor little creature," the man whispered to himself as he thought of the crushed field mouse. He wondered if it still lay there under its tiny mound of earth. "I'm sorry," he begged forgiveness, "I didn't mean to hurt you."

He opened his eyes. The bright ceiling light was not the sun. It did not send down rays of heat to warm him. The room felt cold and the man shivered. He forced his body deeper into the bed. His toes and fingers were numb. He pressed his arms tight against his body. A stream of icy air seemed to be flowing into the bed. He lay his hands on his abdomen, then jerked them away. His chilled fingers sent shudders rolling through his body. Deep inside his belly a movement started. He tensed, gathering all his strength for the coming battle. Then with a racking sigh he let his muscles grow soft again. "What's the use?" he whispered. "The hell with it."

The movement in his abdomen grew stronger. "So that's it," the man groaned, remembering the scratching of the mouse as it struggled to free itself. "You win," he sobbed, "you win." The sound of the siren began to roar in his ears. They were carrying Mr. Tannenbaum, the old man from upstairs, into the ambulance. They slid the stretcher into the dark of the vehicle, then slammed the doors.

# 46

As soon as the defibrillation machine had been wheeled out, the orderly, at a signal from the male nurse, entered the man's room. Although the body had been replaced in the bed from the floor where it had been worked on by the emergency team, the room, by its wildly disordered state, still gave stark evidence of the frantic efforts at resuscitation. Tightening his stomach muscles against the shudder he always experienced when confronting a patient who had just died, the orderly started doing what was required of him. He kept his eyes away from the wasted face that still showed traces of the final desperate moments.

Outside in the hallway the resident was making some final notations on the man's chart. The intern approached, looking like he had slept in his hospital uniform. "I just heard," the intern said, nodding toward the man's room. "What happened?"

The resident shrugged. "I wish I knew. I thought we had him stabilized, then all of a sudden . . ." He swallowed hard and made a helpless gesture with his hands. "Probably a massive infection—his immune system just gave out." The intern nodded.

"I thought we had him stabilized," the resident said again,

his eyes studying the chart. "I would have given odds we could have kept him going for another couple of months, maybe more. I would have given odds . . ." His voice trailed off.

"Does his wife know?" asked the intern, leaning over the other man's shoulder as he tried to decipher the scrawled notations on the chart.

"Not yet. I asked the head nurse to leave the notification up to me." The resident forced a cough as he tried to relieve a tightness in his throat. "It's better if she hears it from someone she knows." The intern nodded. "And—" The resident hesitated, then sighed. "If we're ever to know what happened we have to take a look inside." The intern continued nodding, as if a clockwork device had been implanted in his head. "I'll try to lay the groundwork over the phone; then when she comes in tomorrow . . ." Without quite realizing what he did, the intern laid his hand on his colleague's shoulder; and in the brief moment it rested there he could feel the tremble his eyes were unable to detect.

"They gonna get that autopsy release one way or the other," the orderly muttered as he heard the two doctors' footsteps receding down the hall. "Can't stand not knowin'." For the first time since entering the room he allowed his eyes to focus on the man's face. "Well why not. Won't make a damn bit of difference to you, man. Not one damn bit of difference." With a skill developed from years of practice he started maneuvering the body from the bed onto the gurney. "Maybe I could of helped you like you said, man." The orderly grunted as he shifted the dead weight. "Maybe like you said, me and two others workin' together coulda done her. But first you had to hang in there, man. Without you hanging in there, ain't nothing I could do. Nothin' anyone could do, man. Nothin'."

225

# 47

The violent thrashing of the baby dragged the woman into wakefulness again despite her bone-deep exhaustion. She rubbed the sleep film from her eyes and then tried to focus them on the luminous dial of the clock, but the effort of looking was just too much. She flexed her legs and tried to settle back down to sleep, her hands unconsciously stroking the taut skin of her abdomen. But sleep wouldn't come. She considered making the effort of dragging herself into the kitchen to prepare a cup of hot cocoa. She had already extricated one leg from the warm covers and was about to free the other when the telephone rang.

In the few seconds it took her to reach the phone in the other room, icy needles formed in the tissue of her hands and feet. As she heard the controlled voice of the resident her lips began to tremble and her tongue felt swollen—too big for her mouth. Afraid her swollen tongue would not work, she started to nod at the carefully formed words; but then when the words stopped, waiting for her to reply, she murmured into the strange instrument, "I'm sure you did everything possible." More words from the instrument, then another pause: "I understand. I'm glad you called me now instead of waiting until morning." More words coming out of that wire leading into the wall. Then again a pause waiting for her words. "Yes, certain papers to sign. Yes, of course, if you think it will aid medical science." More words. "Yes. In the morning. I'll be there in the morning."

Whispering the words "I'll be there in the morning; I'll be there in the morning," the woman lumbered back to the bedroom. Then after falling heavily on the bed she tried to say the words again but they were blocked by a hot pressure at the base of her throat. The hot pressure swelled into a scream, a terrible scream that struggled to release itself but the woman fought it back down, down into the dark liquid of her being where the baby floated now fast asleep.

## ABOUT THE AUTHOR

Daniel Panger is the minister of the First
Unitarian Church of Albuquerque,
New Mexico. He was born in New York City
on May 16, 1926. Before entering the
ministry, he held a variety of jobs, including
juvenile probation officer, door-to-door
salesman, nightclub operator, and
practical nurse. His previous books include
*Ol' Prophet Nat* (a novel) and *Business
and the Hardcore Unemployed.*

## PUBLISHER'S NOTE

Readers of this novel may be interested
to learn that there is an international
movement, based in large part on
volunteer efforts, towards alternatives
to hospitalization for terminally ill persons.
The most visible alternative is the hospice
movement. A directory of hospices in the
United States is available for $5.00 from
the National Hospice Organization,
765 Prospect Street, New Haven,
Connecticut 06511.


This book was edited by Bernard Kamoroff
and Paul Williams, and designed and set
in type by J'Ann Tolman. Printed in the
U.S.A. by Kingsport Press of Kingsport,
Tennessee.

WITHDRAWN